SONG OF SIEGE AND SHADOWS

CLAUDIA KLEIN

Copyright © 2024 by Claudia Klein

Cover Design CoverLove Graphic Designs

All rights reserved.

No portion of this book may be reproduced in any form without written permission from the publisher or author, except as permitted by U.S. copyright law.

This is a work of fiction. Names, characters, places, events and incidents are either the products of the author's imagination or used in a fictitious manner. Any resemblance to persons, living or dead, or actual events is purely coincidental.

CONTENTS

To the dreamers

May all your dreams come true

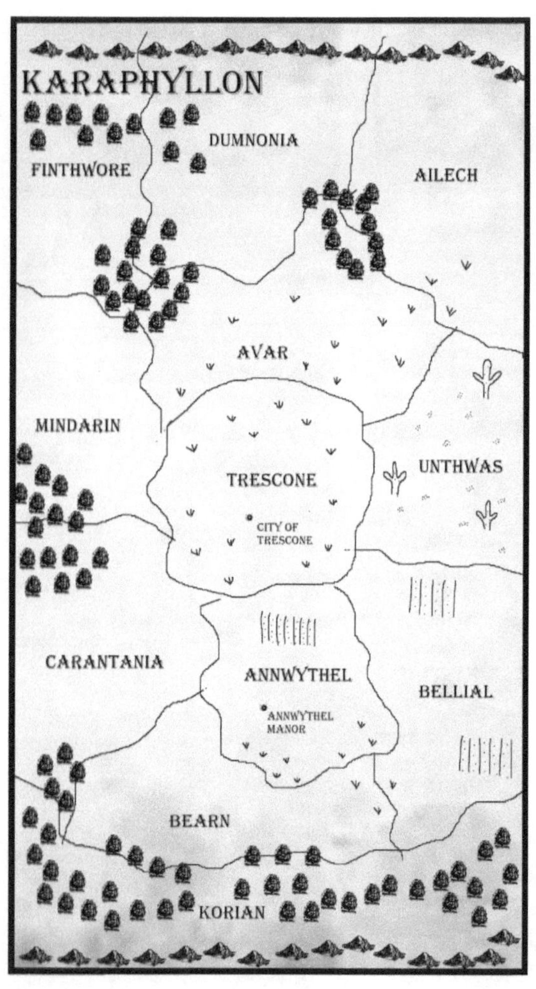

KARAPHYLLON
FINTHWORE
DUMNONIA
AILECH
AVAR
MINDARIN
TRESCONE
UNTHWAS
CITY OF
TRESCONE
CARANTANIA
ANNWYTHEL
BELLIAL
ANNWYTHEL
MANOR
BEARN
KORIAN

ELVISH DICTIONARY

E llas-male Elf

    Ellases-plural of male Elf

Ellassen-female Elf

Ellassens-plural of "female Elf"

Fanwas-boy Elf

Fanwases-plural of "boy Elf"

Fanwassen-girl Elf

Fanwassens-plural of "girl Elf"

Karaphyllon-the planet Elves live on.

Sterathelassa-the Elvish afterlife. It's a land they sail to when their time on Karaphyllon is up.

The Black Lands-The Elvish place of torment. It's where evil creatures that the Mighty One didn't intend to live in Karaphyllon are banished to.

The Mighty One-The Elvish god.

PROLOGUE

CHOOSING DAY

Gwynneth

Choosing Day is the most decisive event in an Elf's lifetime.

I've seen it year in, year out. When ellas masters choose from our fine young fanwases for their apprenticeships. It's how we've always done it here in Karaphyllon, the Living Land, the land of Elves.

"Father says he's going to apprentice me to the king's blacksmith," Timithen said, coming in through the doorway and plopping down on the settee beside me.

He's tall for his age, taller than any of the other fanwases, with long hair hiding his pointed ears. It will need cutting when he starts his apprenticeship. It's all part of becoming an ellas, taking on a trade, cutting your hair short to look like the other ellases. Choosing Day is a big day for fanwases and this year I'm proud that my twin brother is up for his.

I looked up from my needlework, my back aching from trying to sit up straight as I finished this piece. Mother said this was how ladies built endurance. They would grow up to become wives to great lords, like Father, by practicing needlework as young fanwassens. Personally, I think endurance was built on doing hard labor, something that makes you sweaty and sore by the end of the day.

"The king's blacksmith, Carlel?" I asked, gratefully setting down my needle and leaning back against the wall.

"The one and only," he said with a satisfied grin. "I hope he picks me at Choosing Day. It's only a week away. What do you think? Are my arms cut out to be a blacksmith?"

He flexed his bicep, and I realized that he'd put on a little muscle this summer, too. Yet another sign that my twin brother was ready to be chosen and become an ellas. He was growing up.

"But, Gwynneth, I've been thinking," he said, his grin fading and his eyes becoming serious. "You should apprentice to him with me."

I shook my head. "Ellassens aren't allowed to apprentice themselves. You know the rules of society. Ellassens are meant to be homemakers and marry well."

"But you know you'd like to be apprenticed," Timithen said, taking my hand and giving it a tug. "We'll make a fine blacksmith of you, hmm?" His confident smile returned, and I knew he was earnest about this.

He really thought that an ellassen could become apprenticed to a blacksmith. As far as I knew, it was rarely done. Ellassens working an ellas's job just wasn't seen in Karaphyllon. I had never witnessed a master craftsman picking an ellassen as apprentice on Choosing Day. Our world was very old, the Elves of Karaphyllon extremely set in their ways. We'd been doing some things the same way since the Ancient Days, when Elves still spoke the Old Elvish tongue.

I gave Timithen a disbelieving smile. Some things were too lofty to actually achieve. Even things I'd wanted my entire life.

"Any news of the Shadow?" I asked, changing the topic.

Timithen stiffened. Talk of the Shadow was enough to make anyone nervous.

"I might ask Father about that, if I were you." He stood up to go, all merriment swept from his face.

"Why? What did he tell you?" I sighed. Father was always telling Timithen things that he never mentioned to me. It was because Timithen was a fanwas and I was a fanwassen.

"Just...Ask him at supper." He walked off, leaving me puzzling.

"No, absolutely not," Father said, when we pitched Timithen's idea of apprenticing me to the king's blacksmith at supper that night.

All four of us were gathered around the large dining table, using only one end for our little family. Mother sat to Father's right; Timithen and I were across the table on his left.

Father still had on his robes of estate, the uniform he wore as a Lord of the King's Council, when it was in session, which was often. He looked every part an Elf of the nobility as he vehemently shook his head no. His dark hair was cropped short, the way an ellas's hair should be, showing off his finely pointed ears. He was clean-shaven, as all Elves are, his features handsome and wizened.

"I am a Lord of the Council. Leader of the Finthwore Tribe," Father went on. "And you are my children." He looked from one of us to the other, his eyes stern, his voice firm. "Our family has a reputation to keep. We cannot be like every other Elf, wanting modern things for our children. Apprenticeships for ellassens are rarely done, and never among us nobility. An apprenticeship for Gwynneth is outlandish and unheard of. Ellassens do not take on apprenticeships. They don't get chosen. Do not mention this to me again."

"Cedgewick, please don't shut this idea down so hastily," Mother cut in, resting her silverware on her half-eaten plate and looking up at Father, her eyes gentle, as always.

Her long brown hair was coiled high on top of her head while little ringlets framed her face. High cheekbones made her look every part an elegant, knowledgeable Elvish lady. The faint color of the rouge she wore brightened her cheeks, giving her a young, innocent flare. But that was the way with all Elves. Ageless. Beautiful. Wise.

Father snapped his sharp gaze to his wife and his eyes softened. He had a love for my mother that went beyond words. No doubt their marriage was a match made in Sterathelassa by the Mighty One, himself.

"What are your thoughts on it, Mirith?" If Father did anything well, it was to respect the opinion of his wife, ellassen though she may be.

"Apprenticing Gwynneth to Carlel would be a good learning experience for her," Mother said slowly, thinking as she spoke. "What if the Mighty One convicts you to make your journey to Sterathelassa before Gwynneth is out of our home? What will become of her then? I don't want my daughter to become yet another unskilled el-lassen, unable to support herself if the ellases in her family were to pass on to Sterathelassa before their time. I think learning this trade is a good thing for Gwynneth."

Sterathelassa, the Land Beyond the Sea. The final home of all the Elves. Every time Mother spoke of it, a longing stirred inside of me, yearning for something we didn't ex-perience in Karaphyllon. Something inexplicable. Home. Rest. Peace.

"I'll think about it," Father said. Even his tone of voice was softer now, not as harsh. "Now. Can we turn this conversation to something else?"

I cleared my throat. "Father, what news of the Shadow?" I clutched my napkin nervously in my left hand, afraid he wouldn't tell me.

Everyone at the table became more alert as I broached the topic. The Shadow was just a rumor, whisperings of frightened stable boys and uneducated farm hands. An invisible sliver of evil sweeping a fingernail of darkness through our peaceful land.

"I haven't heard anything recently," Father murmured.

"But Timithen said—"

"And Timithen will be an ellas in a few days. He knows when to keep his mouth shut about private conversations," Father said, giving a pointed look at my brother.

Timithen colored and looked down at his plate.

"Yes, Father," I said, inwardly sighing.

"Now, can we speak of happier things?" Father said. It wasn't a question.

I felt the tension in the room ease as we forced ourselves to think of less heavy subjects. We spoke lightly of other things like my lessons in the school for ellassens, the latest technique the sword master had taught Timithen, and Mother's tea today with Queen Arriel. The topic didn't return to Timithen's upcoming apprenticeship and the possibility of me being chosen with him. That was how it was in our house. Father's will was law.

I went to bed that night hoping that Father would relent and allow me to become a blacksmith.

⟡

"I'm so excited about tomorrow, I don't know how I'll sleep tonight," Timithen said.

It was the night before Choosing Day and he had sneaked into my room before bed. One last talk before the big day. One last word with his twin sister before he became an ellas. Now we sat in my window seat, chatting like schoolchildren.

"I'm excited for you," I said with a grin. "You'll be considered an ellas and I'll be considered an ellassen after tomorrow. It's an important day for our household."

We hadn't heard anything more about me being apprenticed to the blacksmith, too. The more I thought about it, the more I wanted it. It was better than going to the school for young ellassens to learn homemaking skills, then waiting for the right ellas to come along and become his wife. For once, I wanted to do something for myself. Something that would ensure my independence in this world.

Just then, there was a knock at our front door. We turned to each other, open-mouthed. It was after dark.

Who would stop by our house after the evening meal? Elves didn't do that in Karaphyllon.

We heard the muffled sounds of Father answering our front door and showing someone into his study, which lay right off the main hall downstairs.

"It's Carlel. I'd know his voice anywhere," Timithen said, moving to the grate in my floor and pressing his ear against it to hear whatever conversation was going on downstairs. I quickly joined him, and we listened to the disjointed words together.

My heart skittered in my chest when I heard my name mentioned then the words "Choosing Day" and "apprentice." I looked up at Timithen, who was staring at me wide-eyed, a grin spreading across his face.

"Think he's going to choose you, Gwynn?" His blue eyes danced.

He would know better than I what was being discussed between Carlel and Father, going out in the streets like he did. Mother had me staying at home more this week to practice my needlepoint and knitting. I hadn't heard any news about our previous dinner conversation.

We listened in a few more minutes, but since my room wasn't directly above the study, we couldn't really hear anything, just muffled voices and a word here and there.

"Timithen, Gwynneth, come down," Father's voice rang up the stairs, and we scrambled down the narrow flight of steps where he stood with Carlel by his study door.

He looked stern yet determined. I couldn't tell what they'd decided from his expression, and I swallowed the lump of fear in my throat as Timithen and I joined them in Father's study.

"Well, my daughter, your persistence has won in the end. Both Timithen and yourself begin your apprenticeship with Carlel after Choosing Day tomorrow." His words sounded like little musical bells pealing joyfully in my ears.

Timithen grabbed my hands, and we jigged around the room, whooping in delight. Father and Carlel quickly stopped our childish glee.

"That's no way for young apprentices to behave," the old smithy told us, his eyes sharp, yet kind.

My face burned with shame, and I looked down at my slippers. Then I looked up and saw Timithen's eyes dancing with mirth. We would be apprenticed. Together.

⸻⊰❖⊱⸻

Choosing Day came. We made our way to the public square in Trescone, the capital city of Karaphyllon, where we lived. Though Father had a manor in our home province of Finthwore, he never brought us there. Our home was here, in Trescone, among the other Elves living nearest to the king.

The square was crowded. A small stage sat on the edge of the far side of the square, meant for the organizer of Choosing Day to make the announcements and for each master to name the apprentice he'd chosen. The Elves who'd come out for Choosing Day milled in the square around the stage.

Excited young fanwases, about to be chosen for apprenticeship, stood about with their families nearby. They fidgeted and twitched, as if they would rather be running around playing, but they were about to become ellases. Running around like little fanwases was not something they wanted their new masters to see.

Anxious ellassens and proud ellases hovered around the fanwases. The parents ready to hear whether the masters they'd been interviewing with would pick their sons.

Bonthwas, the head of the Craftsman's Guild, stepped up to the stage and began the ceremony.

His speech was short and to the point. There were so many craftsmen choosing apprentices this year, he had to get to the choosing part of the ceremony fast. Otherwise, we'd stand here all day.

I stood next to Timithen, wringing the sides of my dress with my hands. I knew Carlel had come to our house last night to let us know he was choosing me too, but a part of me doubted that it would happen. An ellassen had never been selected during Choosing Day, not from the history of Karaphyllon that I knew of. If they were chosen, it was quietly without all the pomp and circumstance of Choosing Day.

The first of the craftsmen walked up to the podium and announced who he'd chosen as his apprentice. The young fanwas, now considered an ellas, walked up to his new master, and the two walked off into the crowd together, most likely headed to the craftsman's shop. Then the second craftsman made his announcement. Then the third, the fourth.

Timithen shifted from one foot to the other, back and forth, back and forth, as we awaited Carlel's turn at the podium. He was anxious too, but not as nervous as I was. He would be chosen. Whether I would be chosen or not was still up in the air.

Then it was Carlel's turn. The older Elf walked up to the podium, his limp from a war long ago evident in his steps. He had cleaned up well for the occasion, wearing plain clothes that fit his station in life, obviously having taken a bath. His silver hair, worn long like the Elves in the Ancient Days, was pulled back in its usual ponytail. In a way, Carlel clung to tradition, refusing to keep up with the modern trend of cutting his hair short.

He cleared his throat, giving Timithen and I a glance, then turned to address the crowd.

"For my apprentices this year, I choose Timithen, Lord Cedgewick's son."

The crowd began its usual applause. Carlel placed a hand up to quiet them, signifying that he was taking on more than one apprentice.

I held my breath, staring at Carlel wide-eyed, still unable to believe the words I hoped would come out of his mouth.

"I also choose Gwynneth, Lord Cedgewick's daughter, as my apprentice," he finished. Then he stepped off the podium and walked over to collect us, ignoring the gasp of the shocked crowd, his eyes firmly planted on our little family, ready to complete his duty as a master who had just chosen his apprentices.

The backlash of the city wasn't as bad as Father had feared. Perhaps the Elves of Trescone were ready to move on with the way of the world.

Timithen and I started our apprenticeship with Carlel, eager and ready to learn. We called him Master now. It was an exciting time for me, being the first ellassen ever in the recent history of Karaphyllon to be apprenticed to a craftsman to take on an ellas career. But my excitement didn't last long.

We were apprenticed only about six weeks when the fire happened. I had stayed home from work that day, sick with a bad sore throat, which would have just worsened by the smoke from the forge. Timithen went to the smithy without me and we expected him home for lunch. Lunchtime came and went and Timithen didn't come home. After waiting for him an hour, my mother went to the blacksmith shop to see what kept Timithen.

I heard the explosion from our house, which was several blocks away from the blacksmith's. I don't know how it happened exactly. All I know is that the entire blacksmith shop exploded, taking my brother and mother with it. Somehow, Master Carlel lived through it, so, for him, all was not lost. But for me and my father, it was the end of our world as we knew it.

We spent the allotted days mourning. When that time came to an end, we were supposed to resume our regular daily activities, but it was hard, incredibly hard.

I was numb inside, moving through the motions of daily life, not really present. I had lost my entire world. Almost. At least I still had Father and my apprenticeship.

During the two weeks of mourning, Master Carlel had enough time to set up his smith shop again. Instead of rebuilding, King Ethele had moved him into an old two-story shed behind the palace.

I remember that first day back at the blacksmith shop, walking there alone, nearly blinded by tears that I could not blink back. That morning, I went about my usual chores. I felt like I was in a dream, my hands moving automatically. Thankful that I already knew what to do, I found the work easier than I thought it would be. In the afternoon, Master Carlel had me do the usual things, but he added several chores that had been my brother's. I began choking up during the first of Timithen's chores and was full out sobbing by the second chore. Master Carlel finally had pity on me in my distress and sent me home two hours early.

The second day back was a little better. And each day that followed got easier, ever so slightly. Both Father and I were easing out of the darkness of our loss and beginning to move on with our lives. A year passed. Then another. Memories of Timithen and my mother began to fade, and I caught myself unable to remember their faces.

I moved on. Blacksmithing became my passion. I buried myself in my work, eager to learn, eager to help Master Carlel. I needed this apprenticeship. I needed to finish this thing I had started, for Timithen's sake, if not for my own.

CHAPTER I

THE SHADOW

Three years later

Gwynneth

He has come. With him, he brings creatures that do his bidding; Throes from the Black Lands that don't belong here, with the bodies of men and the heads of wolves. Everywhere he goes, death follows him. We have named him Gorion, meaning death, because that is what he is.

The Shadow we spoke of years ago while gathered around the table, those whispers of a darkness creeping through our land, has come to fruition. In him. He has already brought half our little land underneath his shadow. Karaphyllon, the Living Land, the world of us Elves, the world I hold so dear to my heart, for it is the only life I know. No one has withstood against Gorion, and I'm beginning to think that no one can. Surely there must be someone who can defeat him.

"King Ethele has called all able-bodied Elf warriors to the capital to form an army, Gwynneth," Father told me. His voice sounded hopeful.

It was late evening, and we were just about to retire to bed. He sat in his armchair in the parlor, relaxing after a long day's work at the palace before he retired to bed. He had changed out of his state robes and wore the elegant clothes of a noble Elf. His breeches reached to his knees, followed by high socks and square-toed shoes with elaborate buckles. A black jacket with big brass buttons covered his white shirt. Honestly, I thought his state robes looked more comfortable than what we of the Finthwore Tribe wore while relaxing.

Father is a Lord of the Council, the most important Elvish governing body there is next to the king of Karaphyllon. He spends long days at the palace, talking politics with King Ethele and the ten other council members. I was glad he was home tonight and not working late. Father's position in the government is the reason I know so much about Gorion, the monster from the Black Lands who was not supposed to be able to enter our world, yet did. And it's why I'm so afraid.

We sat in our little parlor as we did every night he was home, the candles lit on each of the end tables near our chairs. Their light was just enough to read by, a flickering cheeriness in complete contrast to the darkness Father talked of.

I looked up from the book I held in my lap, instantly alert and ready to hear what other news Father had to say about the war that would soon take place. My fingers holding the book trembled. I didn't like feeling frightened, but the prospect of war coming to our little land scared me to death. Karaphyllon hadn't been in a war since the Ancient Days. Not a war led by an outside invasion. The king's Treasure had kept our land hidden and safe all these years. It wasn't a good sign that the magic the Treasure held seemed to be fading, if it had allowed this Gorion from the Black Lands to enter our world.

"What else, Father?" I asked, tucking my long brown hair behind my pointed ears, afraid to ask, but needing to know all the same.

"Gorion's movements seem to be taking him closer and closer here to Trescone," Father went on. "King Ethele believes it is here we will make our stand against Gorion to utterly defeat him."

Trescone is the capital of Karaphyllon, surrounded by the eleven provinces. Each province belonging to an Elf Tribe, each tribe ruled by a lord. Trescone, which sits in the center of our world, is where the king, the Chief Tribeless, lives and rules our world with a benevolent and just hand. The Tribeless, the top of the Elvish nobility, is what each Elf desires to become, but it is denied to many of us. And now this Gorion marches on our capital, to wage war on our mighty Tribeless king.

"Surely if all able-bodied warriors in Karaphyllon join to fight against him, we'll be able to overcome him. Right, Father?"

"That is my hope, Gwynneth," he answered with a small smile. "The entire council is meeting later this week to discuss the king's plans. I might be busier than normal. I wanted to let you know. Now, off to bed with you. It's been a long day and we're all tired. I'll be turning in shortly myself."

I trudged up to bed, weary from the day's work at the smithy. I'm still an apprentice to Carlel, one of the city's most esteemed blacksmiths. Now, in the third and final year of my apprenticeship, at age eighteen, I'll be getting my certificate of completion soon. Just a few more weeks of work, and I'll be able to start up my own forge if I so desire.

These days, the king kept us busy making weapons as he prepares our troops for this oncoming war. Weapons are the one thing we lack, being a peaceful nation. But the thing we need most now. Each ellas has trained with the sword, but whether they own one is debatable. I'm glad I can work in this way, supplying a need in our land.

As I unbuttoned my shoes and took off my stockings, I shook my head once again, marveling that I was taking on an ellas's trade. It's not something a typical ellassen does. Typically, ellassens learn how to keep house, manage accounts, sewing and the like; all the gentle arts that a good ellassen wishing to marry and raise a family might learn. I was not a typical ellassen. Timithen had seen to that, begging Father to let me join him in his trade. For that, I was forever grateful.

I washed my face and hands in the little washbasin by the window, trying to picture my loved ones. If only Father had gotten one more family painting done before they passed. But all I had to go off of was an old painting that hung in our stairwell. It was done when I was just ten years old, back in the days when Timithen still wore his hair long, like a fanwas. Before Choosing Day, before we became ellas and ellassen.

I pulled back the covers and got into bed. Blowing out the candle, I tried to quiet my mind so I could fall into my dreams. Elves do not sleep like I have heard mortals in other worlds do. We dream of a life lived long ago, or a life we have yet to live. No one knows which.

It was a busy day ahead, back to the smithy for me and back to the council for Father. They were occupied preparing for that thing I feared most: war.

Alec

I noticed the storm clouds rising in the distance. They seemed darker than usual, as if some unseen source urged the storm to become more violent than it intended to be. Gripping my reins a little tighter, I guided my horse along the dirt road. The great plains surrounded me, the grasses swaying and bending in the wind. I was heading toward Trescone. As a Lord of the Council, I was called there often these days for matters of business.

With war against Gorion imminent, it was my job, along with the ten other lords and King Ethele, to make sure that this creature's dark magic didn't swallow up our little land.

But something more awaited me in Trescone this time than just boring meetings and trying to persuade the older, stuffy members of the council to listen to my youthful ideas. Something that I felt was my destiny.

⸺❖⸺

Gwynneth

"Gwynneth, I'd like you to come home early from the smithy today," Father told me at breakfast the next morning.

"Why, Father? Is something important happening this evening?" I asked, looking up from my plate of eggs and fruit. I hoped it had nothing to do with the threat of Gorion marching to attack our city.

"I'd just like you to come home early. That's all," he repeated, the slightest gleam of secrecy in his brown eyes.

He wore his hair short like every respectable ellas in Karaphyllon, the dark brown turning to silver at the temples. It fell in thick waves to just above the collar of his long tunic. The rich gray robes fell open in the front, revealing the white shirt and black breeches he wore underneath. A beautiful, flowing pattern of darker gray embroidery adorned the sides and back of the robe.

"All right, I'll try," I said, not bothering to press him about why, even though I was curious.

From his tone of voice, I knew whatever he wanted me home for was not because of the imminent danger. My father is a man of few words, being one of King Ethele's chief advisers. He knows when to speak and when to be silent. I knew if he wasn't sharing more details, he wasn't willing to share them right now. I'd have to find out later today.

"But I can't make any promises," I added. "Master Carlel has me working all day long. I barely get a bite to eat midday as it is. I'll let him know you requested it, though. No doubt he'll honor your wishes."

"Good," Father said, taking another sip of his coffee. He knew he was an important enough Elf in Trescone for my master to obey him, no questions asked.

He pushed his chair back, wiped his hands on his napkin one more time, and gave me one last smile before he left the house to go work in the palace. He looked tired. King Ethele kept him very busy these days, preparing the entire city for the oncoming battle. Worry lines had begun to make their way across his forehead. If Mother and Timithen's deaths hadn't aged him three years ago, this impending threat had. We may be immortal, but sadness and uncertainty can age us, despite our ageless lives.

I finished up my own breakfast, packed my lunch, and headed to the smithy. I was glad that despite the threat of Gorion brewing, Father still let me walk by myself to the forge. We began to hear rumors of this creature, Gorion, who had entered Karaphyllon from the Black Lands several weeks ago. How he got here, no one knew. We all thought that the evil creatures who inhabited the Black Lands couldn't come here to Karaphyllon. The Mighty One Himself had banished them to the Black Lands, or so we'd thought. Until now.

The Mighty One is the One Power that we believe in. He was a person once; a Great Elf Lord that used to dwell here in Karaphyllon with us. He came millennia ago to the world to dwell among us and teach us how to live upright lives. Telling us He had created our world of Karaphyllon. That He had placed each of us here for a purpose, and one day, we would be welcome in Sterathelassa, the afterlife, to dwell there forever in perfect peace.

The Mighty One left Karaphyllon over six thousand years ago, bringing an end to the Ancient Days and moving us into the modern era. No one knows where he went. He just seemed to have disappeared. Then Elves began saying that he had gone to Sterathelassa to prepare it for us.

It was King Sterran, King Ethele's father, who had discovered the Message the Mighty One had left us. It was directions to Sterathelassa. By sailing across the sea, following the coordinates in the Message, we would land upon those blissful shores and reunite with the Mighty One at last.

Along with the Message was the Treasure. This Treasure the Mighty One made for us to protect Karaphyllon in His absence. He had always stopped evil creatures from other worlds, as well as the Black Lands, from discovering our world. Now the magic in the Treasure would do that work for us. The instructions were to hide the Treasure to keep it safe. In return, its magic would protect us for generations to come. Every time a new king took the throne, the Treasure was to be located and hidden again by the new king to keep its location from ever being found by our enemies.

We don't use magic in Karaphyllon much anymore, except in my line of work: creation. It's especially never used for defense against evil forces, like it was in the Ancient Days, before the Mighty One walked among us. There haven't been evil forces like Gorion threatening us for thousands of years. Not since before the Mighty One walked among us and brought peace to our land. We have forgotten that kind of magic.

There's so much to worry about with the threat of Gorion, and Father bringing back bad news about his movements toward Trescone every night. In the meantime, I must carry on with my work, making as many weapons at the smithy as I can before Gorion and his army of evil creatures arrive here. But even with all the work I have every day, I still have too much time alone to ponder what will become of us if Gorion takes control of Trescone in the end. I hope that day never comes. Or if it comes, I am no longer here to witness it. I can't imagine a world where Elves don't have the freedom to govern themselves but are instead slaves to someone else.

It was a bright and blustery day as I walked to the smithy. Being the beginning of harvest season in the fields of the provinces surrounding Trescone, there was a definite nip in the air, giving hints of autumn coming. I was glad I'd worn a cardigan today. But goodness knows I'd quickly take it off when I got working in the shop.

I have a very hot and tedious job, but I enjoy every aspect of it. Even though I've become accustomed to it, blacksmithing is hard work that leaves me extremely sore and tired. I would have given up on it years ago if it wasn't satisfying. Anything I make I can sell for a profit. I will never be without a job in any town. Learning an ellas's trade was a much better idea than pursuing a normal ellassen's life.

Usually, ellassens go to school until they're sixteen. At that point, they are either formally betrothed to a young ellas, or they stay at home with their parents and wait until such an ellas comes knocking at their door. To keep busy, most ellassens learn a great deal of homemaking skills, which are good to know. But I knew that my lot in life would not involve being a homemaker for some ellas. And remaining with my parents to learn homemaking is just silly.

I knew I would never marry by the time I was fourteen. I scared away most of the fanwases who thought to look twice at me. Father has always seen that and worried about me.

No respectable ellassen chooses not to marry. Especially one of the nobility, like myself. It's just expected of one to marry an ellas who will provide for you, and produce his heirs. But I've never desired that kind of life, nor met an ellas that I ever thought I could spend the rest of my life in harmony with, other than Timithen, but he was my brother and that doesn't really count. No, I shall remain a single ellassen, blacksmithing till my dying breath, I am sure of it. Especially now that my apprenticeship with Master Carlel is nearly at an end.

I turned the corner and walked into the smithy, happy to be at work and to be able to quiet my mind with the steady pounding of my hammer.

CHAPTER 2

A Handsome Stranger

Gwynneth

When I arrived at the smithy, Master Carlel wasn't there. Being in the third and final year of my apprenticeship, I knew how to get the smithy up and running without him, so I got to work.

Making my way to the bellows, I fanned the few glowing orange coals that remained in the forge from yesterday's work, using an incantation to speed up the process. Within a matter of seconds, I had a small flame going to which I added more fuel, and cast the spell to make it into a fire hot enough for our work that day.

I then went over to Master Carlel's daily work log, a small leatherbound notebook on the corner table, and looked at what he had us scheduled to do. He wanted me to finish beating down and shaping the long lengths of steel that we received from the steel smith.

I sighed and looked at the still large pile of unworked steel in the corner. Sword making isn't exactly boring, but the kind of sword making that we were doing was. Most of the time, when blacksmiths make swords, they personalize them. Spending hours of extra, detailed work to inscribe information about the soldier who was to carry the sword. It was something we enjoyed using magic for. We enjoyed spending the time making someone's sword special for them. But, since we didn't know who would be using these swords, we didn't take the steps to personalize them.

Instead, I was to beat down the main sword piece, and Master Carlel had taken on the task of making the cross-guards and pommels. Working in more of an assembly line, we found, was faster than what we usually did; each of us working on our own swords from start to finish.

Disappointment filled my heart when he told me we were making plain, solid swords, using magic for speed instead of beauty. We'd need enough swords to outfit an entire army of soldiers who may or may not have a sword of their own.

A half hour passed, and Master Carlel still hadn't arrived. Since I knew how to do everything, including all the magic involved in sword smithing, I didn't waste any time getting started with the work. I'd been pounding away at a sword for a good twenty minutes when someone clearing their throat in between my swings, startled me. I whirled around to find the handsomest young ellas I'd ever seen standing in the shop's doorway.

His eyes were a startling blue that shone from his tanned face. He had high cheekbones, like most of us Elves, that fell into a rich mouth with a pointed, clean-shaven chin. His dark brown hair was cropped shorter than my father's, the ends just about to touch the tips of his pointed ears. He wore a black shirt loosely on his muscled torso, and his matching black trousers and leather dress shoes completed his ensemble. I could tell instantly from his hairstyle and clothes that he was from the Annwythel Tribe, and I wondered if he lived here in Trescone or if he was from Annwythel Province. He was too tanned to belong here in Trescone, where we Elves spent most of our time indoors.

He looked just as startled to see me here as I was at his sneaking up on me. He looked me up and down from head to toe and took in my leather work apron and the hammer I held firmly in my hand. Then his eyes searched around the shop, obviously looking for an ellas smithy.

"You're not Carlel, are you?" he asked hesitantly. His voice was low, mellow, and smooth as silk.

I smiled warmly at him. "No, my master hasn't arrived for the day's work yet. Can I help you with anything?" I asked.

"Do you work here?" His eyes still darted around the shop, looking for another Elf. I knew he struggled to believe that an ellassen was working in a blacksmith shop all by herself.

"Yes, I'm Carlel's apprentice," I answered politely. Over the years, I'd had many encounters with ellases who didn't think it was possible that I could work here, and I'd learned not to take offense at their narrow-mindedness and instead treated them as politely as I could. "Do you need help with anything?" I repeated my question.

"Well, maybe I'll wait for Carlel to get here," he said warily.

"Look, I've been apprenticed here the past three years. My apprenticeship is almost completed," I said, placing my hands on my hips while still holding my hammer. "If there's anything you need done, I can probably do it for you. And if I can't, you can drop it off here and I'll let Master Carlel know about it so he can get to work on it when he arrives." I'd seen this excuse too, and my patience was still holding out well today, thankfully.

"Well, I really don't know how an ellassen—" he started, but that did it for me. I lost my patience and butted in.

"You don't think an ellassen will be able to help you? Is that it?" I asked in a clipped tone. "For your information, sir, my master says that my skills are better than any ellas apprentice he's had at the three-year mark. Thank you very much."

The ellas took a step back, and I instantly felt the heat creep up my neck and into face, embarrassed that I'd let him make me frustrated.

"I'm sorry," I said, looking down.

"No, I'm sorry," he replied. "It's just, I've never met an ellassen who's a blacksmith. Pardon my unbelief in your skills. It was wrong of me. Can I show you what I want done?"

"Sure," I said, looking back up at him. Oh, those blue, blue eyes. And that mouth twisted up in a slight smirk. How handsome he was.

He pulled a sword that hung from his belt out of its sheath and held it up. It was beautiful, skillfully crafted and designed for someone important by the markings that ran all the way up and down it.

"I've never seen such a fine sword," I said as he handed it to me. "It would be an honor to work on something as precious as this."

I spanned my hand down the flat of the blade, admiring the fine details the maker of this sword had put into it. A few of the runes I didn't understand, but they looked like Old Elvish, a language long forgotten.

I could tell at once what work needed to be done on it. Though the sword was still good, well-polished and kept, the hilt was rusting, and in some places, decaying. It had obviously not been made as carefully as the actual sword.

Perhaps the smith who'd made it had used a less pure metal or hadn't preserved it properly for use and hard weather.

"This was my father's sword," he told me. "He gave it to me when I was a young ellas. I've tried to keep it tucked away and safe, seeing as it's a family heirloom. I haven't needed to use a sword in some time. And well, you see, with the impending battle against Gorion, I thought perhaps my father's sword would bring me some luck."

"How do you know about the battle? I thought only the king and the members of the council knew about it," I said.

"The word's all over the capital," he said with a shrug. "It's about the only thing anyone talks about anymore." He paused, my words sinking in. "If only the king was supposed to know about the attack, how did you know?" His gaze narrowed, and I saw a small frown crease his young brow.

"My father is one of the king's chief lords, a member of the council," I answered proudly.

He took a step back, eyes startled. "Then you're..." he began, then stopped.

"I'm what?" I asked, curious at what he had been about to say.

"You're a lord's daughter, then?" he asked.

I could tell that wasn't what he had originally been wanting to say.

"Um, yes. If he's my father, wouldn't that make me his daughter?" I asked, raising my eyebrows in question.

"Oh, of course it would," he said hurriedly, obviously embarrassed. "Anyway, as you can see, the hilt needs replacing."

"Yes, I see that. Any particular type of metal you'd like me to replace it with?"

"Well, what do you suggest?" he asked.

I felt a surge of success that he trusted me enough to ask my opinion, even though he hadn't thought me good enough to do the work a few minutes ago.

"Most of the swords we've been making we've just used normal steel wrapped in shargreen," I said.

"Shargreen?" he asked with a puzzled look.

"A type of leather. It's easier to hold that way. Creates a good grip," I said.

"Ah, well, if you think that's what it needs, then I'd like that," he said.

"Unless you'd like me to leave the hilt uncovered and decorate it?" I asked.

"Um, I'm not sure. Do most people decorate their sword hilts?"

"Well, they usually just inscribe or bejewel the pommel, not the grip. But some ellas like the grip to have something special engraved on it. The name of their spouse, for example," I explained.

"Well, I'm not married, so I guess I don't need anything engraved on the grip," he answered hastily. "Just replace the hilt with whatever you're making these sword hilts with." He indicated the few swords leaning against the shop wall that were still in the progress of being made.

"And keep the pommel the same, since it's still intact?"

"Yes," he said.

"All right. It should be ready by tomorrow. And if not, no later than two days from now," I said, setting the sword down on the bench and getting ready to turn back to my work.

"You're sure you can do this correctly?" he asked, leaning forward, his eyes on his sword.

"Do you see these other swords in here?" I asked, spanning my hand toward the pile of finished swords that lay on the ground in the corner. "I've made them almost all by myself. My master will be here soon to help me, anyway. You have nothing to worry about. Your sword is in good hands, trust me." I gave him a confident smile. A smile usually helped ease ellas minds.

"Well, alright," he said, reluctant to leave.

"Tell you what, I won't touch it until my master arrives and has a look at it. If he doesn't think I'm good enough to do the job right, he'll do it himself."

"Alright," he said with a quick nod. "Sounds good. Thank you, Gwynneth." He turned to walk away.

"Wait, how do you know my name?" I asked, not remembering giving it to him in our conversation.

He turned back, looking startled, almost as if he'd done something wrong. "Oh, um, I don't know. Is that your name?" he asked. His blue gaze held fast to my own, his lips parted in anticipation of my reply.

"Yes," I breathed. The way those blue eyes made my chest all fluttery inside; I felt out of place and flustered under their gaze. "Well, no matter how you know my name, you do," I said, trying to brush it off. But there was so much in a name, at least here in Karaphyllon. "What's your name?" I asked, hoping he'd give it to me willingly.

"Alec," he answered, then walked off.

CHAPTER 3

WE'VE COME TO AN UNDERSTANDING

Gwynneth

I stood there, puzzling over how Alec knew my name. I didn't know him, that was for sure. Perhaps he'd seen me at a social function and had asked one of my friends my name. That had to be it. How else would he have found out? I shrugged it off and got back to work, trying not to let it bother me.

But there was so much in a name. Names were one's essence. Who you were. They were not given easily and not taken lightly. I was so flustered that Alec knew my name without me giving it to him that I worked in a daze until Master Carlel arrived an hour later.

As I'd guessed, the pace of our work quickened tremendously. If Master Carlel did anything, he did it with a sense of urgency. I understood it in this case. Here we were, preparing the weapons for a battle that would determine Karaphyllon's future. If we needed anything, it was haste.

I showed him the sword Alec had dropped off and asked if he felt comfortable with me solely working on it.

"Why, of course, I don't doubt your skill," Master Carlel said, smiling fondly at me. "Just be sure to use as much magic on it as you can to make it go faster. We don't have time to dawdle, even for personal orders."

"Yes, Master Carlel," I agreed, bouncing on the balls of my feet, trying hard to contain my excitement at getting to work on this beautiful sword.

I wondered not for the last time why Alec had looked startled when I'd told him who my father was. It startled many Elves when they found out that one of the chief lord's daughters was a blacksmith's apprentice, but his reaction was different. He'd looked almost bewildered, as if it bothered him personally, when he didn't even know me.

And he'd known my name when I knew for sure that I hadn't told him. Who was he that he knew a lord's daughter's name? Not everyone did. In fact, hardly anyone did. No one needed to bother with knowing my name. It was my father who was important, not me. And, if I held up to tradition, I would just be married off to someone, and live a long, unimportant life somewhere in Karaphyllon, despite being of the nobility. Your station didn't really matter as an ellassen.

When we took a quick break for lunch, I remembered to tell Master Carlel my father's mysterious request to come home early. He smiled mischievously and agreed. I was getting the feeling that he and my father were working together to plan some sort of surprise for me. I couldn't even begin to guess what it was all about. My birthday was nowhere near, nor was any other special occasion that would offer them an excuse to give me a gift or let me do something exciting. There was no sense worrying myself about what waited for me when I got home from work this evening. I would just find out what it was when the time came.

Even though I tried not to think about it, the afternoon seemed to drag on. I was busy working the entire time, thrilled to be working on Alec's beautiful sword as well as the others, but time seemed to stand still. I kept setting my work down to go peek outside and see where the sun stood in the sky as the time grew nearer for me to go home. Master Carlel knew what I was doing each time I walked out. When he usually would have reprimanded me for taking so many quick breaks, today he said nothing. He definitely knew about whatever my father had waiting for me at home. I tried to coax it out of him, but he just smiled at me and refused to answer my questions.

"You'll find out all in good time," was all he would say about it.

Finally, the time came when Master Carlel said I could go home for the day. I threw down my tools and bolted out the door.

Running all the way home, I rushed through the front door and into Father's study, where I knew he would be. I threw the study door open with such force that it banged against the wall as I stood there breathlessly, expecting to see just Father sitting at his desk. The scene I ran in on quite shocked me.

Father wasn't alone in his study. True, he was sitting at his desk as usual, but a young ellas was standing before his desk, hands folded behind his back, short-cropped hair falling just above his long, pointed ears. They had been deep in conversation, but quickly quit talking when I barged in.

"Oh, I'm sorry, Father. I didn't realize you were seeing someone," I quickly apologized, turning bright red all the way to the tips of my ears.

I should have thought to knock before coming in here like this; it was obvious from the closed study door that Father was busy with a client.

Father stared at me from behind his desk, his face stern.

The young ellas turned around.

It was Alec, the Elf I'd met at the forge today.

I stood there, open-mouthed, utterly shocked and surprised. I had no idea this ellas knew my father. What could he and Father have been talking about so earnestly right before I came in?

"Ah, Gwynneth, there you are," Father greeted me, trying to make light of the fact that I had rudely barged into his study and interrupted him while he was in a meeting with someone. "Alec and I were just wondering when you would arrive, and here you are." He gave me a pleasant smile, totally void of my misconduct.

"You know Alec, Father?" I asked, unsure of what else to say.

"Yes, we've been corresponding long distance for quite some time now," he answered. Then, seeing how the two of us were staring at each other, especially me, and my use of Alec's name, he added, "Have you two met already?"

"I dropped off my sword for repairs at her—I mean, Carlel's—blacksmith shop. We met there this morning," Alec replied, briefly taking his eyes off me while he addressed my father, then returned his eager gaze to meet my surprised one.

"Well, how surprising," Father said. "I thought I would have the honor of making the formal introductions."

"You can still do that, sir. She doesn't know who I am yet," Alec answered, pulling his gaze away from me and turning back toward my father, who had risen from his chair and come around to the side of the desk Alec was standing on.

"You didn't tell her?"

"No sir. You told me not to breathe a word of it to anyone, and I'm an ellas of my word," he answered, looking proud of himself.

"Tell me what?" Now I was confused, and a little bewildered.

My father and this ellas, Alec, had been corresponding for some time now. Did that mean Alec wasn't from the capital like I'd suspected at the forge? What did he have to write my father about? A wave of nervousness passed over me and I got the feeling that my life as I knew it was about to change drastically.

"Come here, Gwynneth, my darling," Father said, holding out a welcoming hand to me. "I'd like for you to meet Alec, Annwythel Elf, Lord of the province of Annwythel, and Lord of the Council."

"My, that's quite a title for such a young ellas," I murmured, walking over to stand beside Father at his desk, still confused. Alec gave me a low bow and a breathtakingly handsome smile. "But I see how you know my father now. You're a lord yourself. How have we never met?"

He didn't answer. Merely continued to smile at me in a way that made my stomach turn to butterflies and my heart skitter in my chest. No ellas had dared to look at me like that before. What was going on?

"Alec, this is my daughter, Gwynneth," Father continued.

"It's a pleasure to finally make your acquaintance," he said, addressing me formally, as if we hadn't had that entire conversation at the smithy's earlier today. Honestly, I couldn't make heads or tails of this yet. All I knew was that I was very nervous.

"Now, if you two will be seated, our meeting can begin," Father said, returning to his desk chair and indicating the two wooden chairs that were pulled up in front of the desk.

"I'm confused Father," I said as I slowly sank into my chair, darting a glance at Alec, who was still looking at me with that earnest expression.

"I will explain everything to you now, my dear," Father assured me, folding his hands over his desk. "Now, to business. As I said, Alec and I have been corresponding for a little over a year and we have at last come to an understanding. Do you have any idea what this might be about, Gwynneth?"

The thought of a betrothal darted across my mind for an instant and with it, a sinking feeling. I quickly cleared it from my thoughts.

"No, I wouldn't have the faintest idea why Alec would write to you, Father. Especially from such a long distance. I can't even imagine how he came to know you personally, other than that you're both Lords of the Council," I answered carefully, knowing that Alec was still staring at me with that utterly pleased look of his that was becoming, yet also startling.

"Alec has been inquiring about the possibility, if you consent, of becoming formally betrothed to you. And, if you complete your betrothal, taking you as his wife in holy matrimony," Father said.

A lump instantly formed in my throat, and I willed down the panic rising in my chest. I turned my horrified gaze to Father. I couldn't look at Alec right now. How could Father have done something like this behind my back? He and Alec had been writing about this idea for over a year?

I had sworn to myself that I would never marry. No ellas had wanted to be betrothed to me before, and that must mean that no ellas would ever want to be betrothed to me. I had plans, grand plans, of opening my own smithy and working. Bringing change to Karaphyllon, making ellassens equal with ellases in everything they do.

This was the end for me.

"W-why did you never speak of this to me before?" I asked Father, refusing to look at Alec. I was so—frightened, nervous, panicky—I didn't know quite all what I was feeling at the moment, but nothing good.

"Well, I don't believe in speaking about things like betrothals until it's ready to be finalized. And since Alec lives far away, I didn't want to tell you until he visited and you two met each other," Father explained. How could he speak of this so easily?

"I see," I murmured. All I wanted to do was run out of the room, hide somewhere, and cry, but I refused to give in to my feelings. It was true I didn't want to get married, but it was also true I had to act like a responsible ellassen right now. So, I held my feelings in and put up a brave front.

"And now is the time for you to seriously consider taking this step," Father said encouragingly, smiling at me. He knew nothing of my plans; how this decision of his was about to wreck my entire life.

There was a horribly awkward pause. The room became so silent that the sound of the clock ticking on the mantle sounded like a cannon exploding.

"So, what do you think, Gwynneth?" Alec broke the awful silence, looking over at me. "I know you don't know me very well, but the whole betrothal is a time set aside for us to get to know each other better. I'm very eager to give it a go if you are. Your father has told me much about you, I already feel like I know you quite well."

"Well, I wish he'd told me about you," I replied abruptly, still refusing to look at him. "I'm sorry, I didn't mean to be rude," I said when no one replied. "I just don't know if I'm quite ready."

I kept my eyes focused on a pink rose in the carpet pattern on the floor. To think that I'd thought him the handsomest ellas in Karaphyllon, and now here he was asking to become my betrothed. He was ruining my life. He and Father, both.

It was an all-out lie that I didn't know if I was ready. I knew quite well I wasn't ready. I would never be ready to begin a betrothal with anyone. No matter how handsome the ellas was, or how wonderful his voice sounded to my ears.

I'd decided before I began my apprenticeship that I would never marry anyone. I knew myself well enough to know that I was not cut out for that sort of life. I was happy as I was, on my own, with no one to tie me down, a good job and excellent prospects ahead of me. My future, as I saw it, just didn't have any room for a husband. Why was Father doing this to me?

"It's all right if you need a day or two to think about it," Father said gently. I could feel his steady gaze on me.

I looked up at him and he smiled reassuringly at me, though I saw the concern on his face at my reaction to this. My gaze slid over to Alec for a split second, and I saw the pleading, the desperation, in his eyes. I supposed it hadn't occurred to him that I would refuse his offer. Now he was thinking about that for the first time, and it obviously wasn't a pleasant prospect to him.

I quickly looked back at my father; I couldn't bear to see that almost hurt look in Alec's eyes. Though I didn't know him very well, it didn't feel good that I could hurt him by choosing to refuse him.

"Yes, I think I need some time to think this over. If you don't mind," I said.

"Not at all," Alec quickly replied, clearing his throat. I could hear the nervousness in his voice, the slight falter of the chocolaty smoothness.

"Yes, my dear, take all the time you need," Father added. "In the meantime, Alec will stay here with us for a fortnight or so. Please don't feel you have to take off work at the smithy or anything to entertain him. His journey here was a dual purpose. Not only to meet us but also to attend to the meetings of the council with King Ethele. He'll be quite busy with that during the daytime. In the evenings, you can get to know him a little bit better."

"Yes, Father," I answered, biting my lip.

"That was all I had to discuss with the two of you," Father said, wrapping up our meeting. "Alec, you're welcome to stay in here and either read one of my books or discuss anything else with me. If you're tired, you can go rest in your room, the kitchen, or the parlor."

"Thank you, sir. I think I'll go sit in the parlor for a while," Alec replied. He turned to me, his eyes hopeful. "Would you like to join me, Gwynneth?"

"No," I quickly replied, finally daring to meet his eyes again. He gave me such a warm smile I almost wished I'd said yes. "I'm tired from working all day. If you'll please excuse me."

And with that, I fled to my bedroom.

CHAPTER 4

STUCK

Alec

I walked to the parlor, deflated. That meeting had gone poorly. I had imagined something more than what actually happened.

I knew perhaps it would be a shock to Gwynneth when her father formally introduced us. By the Mighty One, it had been a shock and a half when I'd figured out who she was at the smithy earlier today. Lord Cedgewick had never once mentioned in his letters that Gwynneth was apprenticed to the king's blacksmith. Had he thought that fact unimportant?

Gwynneth had been more than happy to put me in my place earlier at the blacksmith's. True, it was small of me to doubt her skill, but—ellassens were not apprenticed to blacksmiths! What had possessed Lord Cedgewick to allow her to do something that was such an ellas's trade?

I didn't think poorly of her because of it. Rather, I admired her for being brave enough to risk society's disapproval and take on a trade that she obviously enjoyed. It had been nice meeting her at the blacksmith's earlier today.

Taking my seat on one of the plush couches, I looked about the daintily decorated room and smiled, wondering if Gwynneth was the one who had decorated the end tables with doilies and dried flowers. It was such a feminine gesture, something I couldn't imagine the master of this house overseeing.

But that formal introduction! She had looked terrified when her father mentioned betrothal, like she wanted to bolt out of the room. I'd never once pictured that Gwynneth, the ellassen Lord Cedgewick had painted so beautifully in his letters, would react in such a fearful way.

I'd imagined her being polite, like she'd been. Beautiful. She'd been that, too. And I'd imagined her being happy at hearing that a lord like myself wanted to betroth myself to her. That someone with a home and a good position in the government wanted to become her provider. Because that's what I wanted. I felt like I already knew her through her father's correspondence over the past year. I just hoped she'd get to know me well enough to make a decision. At this point, any decision would do, whether she would have me or refuse me.

Gwynneth

Shutting the door safely behind me, I flung myself across my bed and let my pent-up emotions go. The tears came freely, and it felt good to finally let it all out.

Why, oh why, had Father done this to me? Didn't he know I didn't want to get married? I know I'd never said anything against marriage these past three years, but surely he'd seen how stiff I was at the social functions for young ellases and ellassens held here in Trescone. He was always there as a chaperon. Perhaps this was his way of telling me it was time to set aside my trade as a blacksmith and take up my duties as an ellassen.

I knew now that he had never wanted me to be apprenticed to the king's blacksmith. To him, that was a trade meant only for an ellas to work. He'd just done it for Timithen's sake. All these years he'd been letting me follow this pursuit that I loved because he knew how much I missed Timithen. Was this his way of telling me it was time to let my brother go? I couldn't do that, I just couldn't.

Originally, I wanted to do smith-work because that was what Timithen was doing. But over the three years of my apprenticeship, I had grown to love every aspect of the trade. It was a part of me now. Didn't Father see that? How could he ask me to give it up?

I was angry with him, and I hated feeling that way about my father, the only relative I had left in this world. But I couldn't help myself. How could he go behind my back and arrange a marriage for me to a complete stranger? He said I had a choice whether the betrothal would actually happen, but I knew that if it was his wish for me to be betrothed, and eventually marry Alec, I didn't really have a say in the matter. He'd just said that for the sake of formality.

I hated this. I was stuck. Utterly, completely trapped, with no way out that I could see.

I stayed in my room as long as possible. I knew that Collette, our cook, would serve supper in about an hour. Then Father would expect me to come downstairs and join them for the meal. I dreaded seeing Alec again. Not because I didn't like him. In fact, I liked him very much. He was quite an amiable ellas, and we'd had a pleasant conversation earlier at the smithy. It was the fact that I had this choice of agreeing to be betrothed to him or not looming over my head. It would make every minute we spent together very awkward. At least for me.

I spent the remaining time I had before supper sitting huddled up on my bed clutching a pillow to my chest and trying not to let my thoughts get so despairing that I would cry again. If Alec saw me in a disheveled state from crying, I would be mortified. I didn't want him to know how much his offer distressed me.

No matter how hard I tried to think of something else, my thoughts always wandered back to him. I was curious how he had gotten the title of Lord of the Council and Lord of the province of Annwythel at such a young age. He couldn't be much older than twenty-four. In fact, he was probably some years younger than that. He must be the youngest lord in all of Karaphyllon. What had he done early in his life to rise to such a high level?

I watched the minutes slowly tick by on the clock, dreading when the hour hand reached six, which meant I'd have to go down to supper. Five minutes till the hour, I went and looked at myself in the mirror to make sure I didn't look like I'd been crying. There were no traces of my tears, but I poured water in the washbasin and scrubbed my face until it was red, all the same.

The clock struck six, and I waited an entire minute before opening my bedroom door and walking downstairs to the dining room. Father and Alec already sat at the table; Father at the head and Alec placed next to my usual spot. I joined them and we bowed our heads for the silent prayer to the Mighty One before we began to eat the supper our cook, Collette, had prepared for us.

"I hope you feel more rested, Gwynneth," Alec said quietly as he helped himself to the venison roast.

"Yes, I'm very refreshed, thank you," I answered, as he also served me.

I looked down at the food he'd set on my plate. Usually, I would have helped myself like everyone else. I felt my cheeks grow hot, embarrassed that he'd taken the liberty to serve me so casually, as if it was the most natural thing in the world for him to do. We weren't even betrothed yet. What was this ellas thinking?

"Venison roast in the city," he commented. "I never would have imagined that you could find that kind of meat here. Does someone hunt in the fields? There are no woods nearby for miles."

"King Ethele has a particular likeness for fresh venison," Father explained as he cut a small bite of the tender meat. "We receive a portion from the palace kitchen every time the king has it served for his guests. Hopefully you won't grow tired of venison. I have a feeling King Ethele will serve it to you at every meal you take in the palace. He seems to think that if he has important guests at the palace, he should serve them his favorite foods. That includes venison." He politely placed the bite of meat in his mouth. "Ah, excellent, Collette!" he called into the adjoining kitchen. "You've outdone yourself this time. The venison is delicious!"

"Thank you, my lord. I'm pleased to hear that," Collette answered from her post in the kitchen.

"You must be very busy, Lord Cedgewick," Alec said, addressing Father. "I sat all alone in the parlor, thinking at any moment that one of you would join me, but neither of you did."

"Yes, well, King Ethele has me in charge of a good portion of the city's defenses as we prepare to fight this Gorion. These days, I stay up most of the evening in my study doing the king's work. It's what happens during times of war, isn't it? Most of us are kept busy with extra work, preparing for what we hope will never happen."

"Yes," Alec said. "I'm a little nervous about the council meeting tomorrow. I hope whatever the king has to tell us isn't all bad news. Hopefully, we can make plans and solve our problems together, as the council was designed to do."

"I've been wondering Alec," I said, venturing to speak to him. "How are you already in such a prominent position in the land? You seem quite young."

"Well, I think I mentioned my father died when I was very young. I had just become an ellas," he began.

"Oh yes," I said, feeling silly that I hadn't remembered that and put all the pieces together myself.

"When he died, as the eldest son, I became the heir. Upon my sixteenth birthday, I took all my father's titles and his responsibilities as Lord of Annwythel and Lord of the Council."

"That must be quite a burden for you," I said. "Seeing as how you've had little experience."

"On the contrary, I feel very honored to serve my country as a lord of a province and part of the council," Alec said. "I think it's good for all those older lords on the council to have to put up with me and my modern ideas."

"Perhaps not quite so modern," I muttered under my breath, thinking back to the scene in Father's study and his old-fashioned betrothal. True, all Elves still got betrothed before they married. But I haven't heard of an ellassen being betrothed to an Elf she's never met for ages. It's something our parent's generation did that doesn't happen as often anymore. And to think it was happening to me.

"What did you say?" he asked.

"Nothing, I just..." I stopped, unsure of what to say as an excuse.

Alec looked expectantly at me, waiting for me to say something.

"You really think the younger you are, the newer your ideas will be?" I ventured.

"Why yes, don't you?" he asked. "The world is changing, Gwynneth. The old ideas of customs and traditions are becoming a thing of the past. Surely you, of all people, know that. I mean, look at you, apprenticed to a blacksmith."

At that, Father cleared his throat and tried to change the topic of conversation.

"So, um, tell us more about your family, Alec," he said.

Alec, realizing Father's point at interrupting us, answered him easily, making the sudden change of topics a smooth transition.

"Well, sir, there's not much to tell about my living relatives, as there are very few of us," Alec began. "My family's history is long and quite impressive, though. My mother and younger sister are still alive. Other than that, I have no other relatives of noble birth. My uncle on my mother's side is a tanner, and he has a wife and son. That's about it as far as relatives go." Then he turned to me. "You'll like my mother, Gwynneth. She's very kind and has a gentle spirit. And my sister can't wait to meet you. I think you'll like her. You remind me of her, now that I think about it."

To that comment, I said nothing. This was all incredibly awkward. I wished yet again that Father had forewarned me of Alec's visit, and his intentions.

He waited a few seconds for me to respond, then turned back to his supper when he realized I wasn't going to. Glancing his way, I saw the dejected look on his face and the way his shoulders drooped slightly. I felt sorry for him. I wasn't trying to be rude to him. He was being nice, but there was considerable expectation from me. I wasn't handling this very well and was hurting him at the same time.

For the rest of supper, Father and Alec kept up the conversation. They were already such good friends, if you can call a prospective son-in-law your friend. I felt bad for both of them, and ashamed of myself for not wanting to consent to a betrothal with Alec. Father would be disappointed and hurt. Goodness knows how hard and long he'd searched for an eligible husband for me. And here I was, turning my nose up at the prospect.

I breathed a sigh of relief when supper was over, and I stood up to go back to my room.

"Gwynneth, I'd like you to join us in the parlor, if you don't mind," Father said.

He said it as if I had the option to say no, but I knew my father too well; I had no choice. I slowly stood up and stalked away to the parlor. I chose to sit in a low, comfortably upholstered chair instead of the couch. That way, I wouldn't have to sit beside my potential betrothed. Father and Alec followed me into the room and took their seats, Alec on the couch and Father in his usual high-back wing chair.

I grabbed a book that was lying on the end table beside my chair and tried to read it, hoping Father wouldn't attempt to get me to join the conversation. All I wanted was to make my escape for the night up to my room. Part of me wished Father hadn't told me that Alec wished to be betrothed to me. That he'd just let me know Alec was a new friend of his that was going to stay with us for a fortnight. That way, this wouldn't have been awkward, and I might enjoy having a guest in the house for a few days. But there was no changing how Father did things.

I have no idea what Father and Alec talked about during the two hours we sat in that room. Thankfully, I was able to concentrate enough to read my book, and neither Father nor Alec tried to get me to talk to them. When the clock struck ten, I all but ran out of the room and upstairs to bed.

About fifteen minutes later, when I was in my night-gown and about to blow out the candle for the night, I heard a knock on my door. I froze, thinking for a second it was Alec. Then I went to answer the door and Father was standing there in the dark hall, a candle in his hand.

"Gwynneth, I wanted to talk to you for just a minute. May I come in?" he asked.

"Yes, of course, Father," I said, opening the door wider as he stepped into my room. "What is it?"

"I'm quite disappointed in you, Gwynneth. I expected better of you, really, I did," he began.

I ducked my head in shame and said nothing. I'd done quite a terrible job of entertaining our guest tonight.

"I'd like for you to make more of an effort tomorrow to get to know Alec a bit. Surely you didn't act the way you did tonight this morning when you met him at the smithy?"

"No, I didn't. But I didn't know who he was then, either," I said.

"Does knowing that he wants to court you make that much of a difference?"

"Yes, I'm afraid it does," I said, balling my fists at my sides, trying to control my anger toward my father. "It would be one thing if he was just visiting as your friend. But he's visiting as a potential suitor to me, and I don't like it. I wish you'd told me about him earlier, given me time to prepare myself for this. I don't know if I'm ready for this step. I don't know if I'll ever be ready." I said the last sentence in a whisper, but Father still heard it.

"You don't wish to marry?" he asked, his voice etched with a harshness to it that surprised me.

"Father, you know me. I'm not like other ellassens. I've been following an ellas's path for how long now?" I met his eyes and lifted my chin. All that met me back in Father's eyes was sadness.

"But that doesn't mean that you can't marry," he said. "Settle down. Raise a family. Doesn't that sound at all appealing to you?" His voice was gentler this time, and I felt all my pent-up emotions slide away.

"I don't know," I said hesitantly. "I just never thought I'd marry. That's all."

Father stared at me, stiff at my words. "Well, he's here now. And there's nothing we can do to change that," he said, after a moment's silence. "Just try to be friendly. Forget about the possibility of a betrothal and be your normal self. For my sake, if for no one else's, my dear. Can you do that for me?"

"I'll try," I agreed, though I didn't see what good it would make. I'd made up my mind. I wouldn't marry anyone. But I hated to hurt Father so, and the ellas downstairs that he'd picked for me. I just hoped I would make a good decision in the end.

"Good. Well, sweet dreams," he said, giving me a kiss on the forehead.

"Good night, Father."

CHAPTER 5

ISN'T MARRIAGE WHAT ELLASSENS WANT IN THE END?

Gwynneth

That night, it took me a long time to fall into my dreams.

Elves do not sleep. They spend the night hours in a beautiful, waking dream. When I finally fell into my dreams, they weren't pleasant.

I dreamed Father forced me to marry Alec and he and my father made me give up blacksmithing. I was the mother of fourteen children, with no servants to help me care for them. Alec was too busy with his duties as a lord to help me. I lived in a dirty hovel, too busy caring for children to have time to keep the house clean. One by one they all died from the uncleanly conditions.

I jerked out of my dreams with a start. It was morning, and the sun was shining through my window, welcoming the day and washing away the fear of the dream. I shook my head, puzzled. I'd never had a bad dream before. Elves didn't have bad dreams. What was happening to me?

I looked at the clock and realized I'd slept later than usual and if I didn't hurry, I'd be late for work. Pushing aside my troubled dream, I rushed through getting dressed and pulled back my long brown hair into a practical braid. Then I ran downstairs for a quick bite to eat.

There was no sign of either Father or Alec. I breathed a sigh of relief that I didn't have to see them this morning. Last night had been bad enough, and I didn't want to repeat it.

I was soon on my way to the blacksmith shop for yet another day of work. Master Carlel was there when I arrived. He gave me instructions for the morning's work, and we began. Surprisingly, he'd already started up the fire, which was usually a chore I did.

"Were you surprised when you got home yesterday?" Master Carlel asked after we'd been working in silence for a good hour.

"I was flabbergasted," I said. "I wasn't expecting something like that at all." I cast the long piece of steel into the hot flames with my tongs, watching the metal carefully as it heated.

"Were you pleased?" he asked, as he beat the crosspiece he held on the anvil, his rhythm steady, never faltering as he spoke.

"Not really. It caught me off guard," I said, breathing the incantation to get the metal hot enough for working on the anvil. "I was shocked. I'm afraid I was quite rude to Alec last night. How did you know about it, anyway?"

"Your father came by my house last week and told me about the upcoming betrothal. You know, when you become officially betrothed, you won't have as much time to spend helping me out here."

Of course, Father had told Carlel about the impending betrothal. As my master, Carlel was privy to a lot of things that happened with our family, what remained of it. I pushed the dark thoughts of Timithen and Mother's deaths away.

"I think I'll still be able to come to work. I don't think anything is going to happen, anyway." I mumbled the last bit, but Master Carlel still heard me. After all the generations of blacksmiths he'd trained, I knew he really cared about his students and what we thought.

"Oh, really?" he said. I heard concern in his voice but didn't dare look up at my master. "Don't you want to be betrothed?" he pressed, the sound of his hammer never faltering.

"I'm not sure," I lied, pulling the steel from the forge and bringing it over to the anvil. I couldn't even bring myself to tell my master, one of the ellas I trusted most, my plans for singlehood. He wouldn't understand. Remaining single wasn't something ellassens did. "Perhaps if I'd known Alec well before we began a formal betrothal. But I'd never seen him before in my life until yesterday. I'm just pleased I met him before Father introduced us."

"Yes, I was amused that he came by here to drop off that sword, having no idea he would meet you here. He really didn't let on who he was?" Carlel asked, a small smile playing about his lips.

The sound of my master's steady rhythm with his hammer was comforting. I picked up my own hammer and joined him in the song.

"He told me his name. That was all," I said, thinking back to the event. "Come to think of it, he said something strange that left me puzzled. He tried to cover it up. I didn't think much of it at the time. Obviously, he knew who I was, but didn't tell me who he was. Guess he wanted it to be a surprise. My father was the one who was supposed to formally introduce us, anyway."

"So, you're not sure if you want to be betrothed?" Carlel asked, cutting to the chase, as always. "Isn't marriage what all ellassens want in the end? You'd be a strange one not to want that life."

"Yes, well, I haven't always followed others' expectations for an occupation or a way of life now, have I?" I said, indicating the blacksmith shop we were in.

"Yes, that's quite right," he agreed with a proud smile. "I've thoroughly enjoyed having you on as my apprentice. You're worth ten ellases to me. You work just as hard and just as well as they do. You've always impressed me. I might even think about taking on more ellassen apprentices when you leave to start your own practice."

"I'm just grateful the city quieted down soon after I began working for you," I said, thinking back to the wagging tongues that surrounded my family's decision three years ago. I shook my head and smiled. "Where do you think I should go to start up my own smithy? Is there room for me here in the capital?"

"Won't you be going to Annwythel if it all works out with Alec in the end? You should consider having a shop there, since you'll be living there in about a year. If your husband allows it, that is."

"Don't get your hopes up too high, Master Carlel. I already told you I don't like the idea of being betrothed to him. He's a complete stranger to me."

"So, you don't like him at all, then?" Master Carlel asked. "He seems a very agreeable ellas to me."

"I do like him. And he is a very agreeable young ellas. It's just awkward because he and Father are waiting for me to make up my mind about him. There's a great deal of expectation. I don't know if I can live up to it and fulfill both of their hopes. And I hate to hurt him when I barely know him." I pounded the steel with more fury than was good for it, stopping when Carlel gave me a look. I knew better than to be careless in my work. "I can't understand how he can be sure he wants to marry me. He knows nothing about me, other than what Father's told him."

"Perhaps your father told him a great deal about you. Enough for him to be able to make that decision. If he is earnest about being betrothed to you, he must be impressed with you." Carlel gave me a smile that betrayed how proud he was of me himself. "I've heard that lords must choose their wives carefully. They can't just marry any ellassen that first catches their eye. If he's the type of lord I'm guessing he is, he's spent a long time, several years, seeking the right ellassen to settle down with and marry. You should feel honored that he's chosen you."

"I think I do, a little," I said. "It's just...a hard decision to make, that's all. I don't know what I'm going to do."

"Well, whatever you decide in the end, your father will have to honor it. He can't force you to do something you don't want to." Master Carlel dunked the crossguard piece in the cooling tank, then picked up another unworked crossguard.

"Are you sure about that?" I asked, addressing his statement. "Because I feel like I have little say in the matter. Father has obviously found Alec to be highly favorable and wishes that I marry him. I don't think he cares about how I feel about it." I paused in my hammering, saddened by my words. But I knew they were true. "No, Father will arrange a betrothal at the end of Alec's stay here and he'll force me to marry him in the end, no matter what I really want to do," I continued, shaking my head. "I can't imagine leaving the capital. It's been my home my whole life. Father doesn't care for his family to live in our home province. And I'm sure Alec won't want me to continue this blacksmithing trade. You should have seen the way he carried on when he was here at the smithy, unsure if I was capable of repairing his sword." I smirked.

"I'm sure you put him in his place. I've seen you do it to other ellases. It's quite a sight to see them crawl meekly away from you after you correct them for their narrow-mindedness," Carlel said, chuckling, though his eyes were sad from hearing the rest of my thoughts.

"Mhm," I said, ignoring our shared gloominess. "He was reluctant to leave the sword with me, but he did in the end. I'm afraid I lost my temper over it. I'm surprised that didn't make him change his mind about me," I said.

"Lots of ellases like ellassens with a bit of spirit. I preferred it myself, back when I was a young ellas and my wife was alive." He smiled, lost in thought for a minute. "Even if a less spirited ellassen would be easier to get along with," he added, turning back to his work.

"I'm sure you're right. I'll lose in the end, be forced to betroth and marry him, and move far away from here."

"Even if you do move, don't give up hope that you won't ever get to smith again," Master Carlel said, laying a reassuring hand on my shoulder. "You're better than most ellases at the trade and you deserve to have your own shop."

"Thank you. But if you'd met Alec, I think you would agree with me that he's not the sort of ellas that would want his wife working a trade like mine."

"Well, don't give up quite yet. You still don't know what's going to happen," Carlel said. "And since he might end up being your husband, I'm delighted to let you to handle the repairs on his sword by yourself."

I couldn't help but press my lips together and smile at that. I was excited to have the opportunity to work on his sword.

"If you decide before you finish the repair to agree to the betrothal, I'd add your own special mark on the hilt if I were you," he said with a wink.

I laughed. "I doubt I'll be doing that."

"So, you've already decided what your answer will be?"

"Yes, but it won't make any difference."

"Then go ahead and make the mark on the hilt."

"I'll think about it. Can I work on it now?"

"No, we have too many projects the king has given us. You'll have to repair Alec's sword on your own time, I'm afraid."

"You mean spend extra hours working here?" I asked, my hopes rising. Perhaps I wouldn't have to spend as much time back at the house entertaining Alec if I had the excuse that I had to fix his sword before he left.

"Yes, that's what I mean," Master Carlel said, a knowing twinkle in his eyes. "If Alec staying in your home is as awkward for you as you make it out to be, you have my permission to escape spending time with him by working here."

"Thank you, Master Carlel. I appreciate it." I said, beaming.

I continued my work, pounding away at the metal with an added ferocity. Even though I think Master Carlel wanted me to marry Alec in the end, he was taking my side while I was trying to decide about agreeing to the betrothal. And I was thankful to him for that.

CHAPTER 6

THE COUNCIL OF TRESCONE

Alec

"Let the meeting of the council come to order," Jirieth, the Speaker of the Council, called the meeting to order. "King Ethele, you may speak." He nodded to the king to begin.

King Ethele was the head of the Chief Tribeless, the twelfth and last tribe in Karaphyllon. He ruled all of Karaphyllon, uniting the eleven other tribes under the Tribeless banner. The Tribeless's power was given to them by the Mighty One Himself. It was one of His last acts when he'd moved on from our world to Sterathelassa, the Land Beyond the Sea.

The gray-haired king stood, his back straight, his eyes steady as he met each of the lord's faces before speaking.

"You know why I have called you all here," he began.

Gray and white-haired heads nodded around the room. I was one of the few Elves in the room who still had colored hair. That's how much younger I was than the rest of these ellases who led our world. I took my father's place five years ago, and I still felt inadequate to the position among all these older Elves. I didn't deserve it, not with the secret my family was hiding.

"What is your plan for this imminent threat of the monster we have named Gorion, Your Majesty?" Rinion, one of the two white-haired Elves in the room, asked.

Elves' hair turns white around the time they have lived five hundred years on Karaphyllon. It is around the time many choose to make their journey to Sterathelassa. I've known Rinion and I've known him to have white hair the entire span of my life. I wonder every time I see him when he will give up his seat as Lord of the Korion Tribe and give it to his son. His son's hair was already graying. Surely Rinion must give it up soon.

"The plan is simple," King Ethele said, sitting back in his chair that was so ornate it was practically a throne. "I need every one of you to call the warriors of your tribes here to the capital. Our sources tell us that Gorion is heading here. It is here where we will make our last stand. It is here where we will send this monster and his armies back to the gates of the Black Lands where they belong." He pressed his pointer finger on the table for emphasis and his eyes roved from face to face once more. Half of the lords wouldn't meet his eyes.

"On the contrary, Your Majesty, I believe it's better to keep our warriors stationed where they are," Tulese, the Lord of the Mindarin Tribe, said. Though he looked down at the long table as he spoke, his voice was firm with conviction. "Gorion first appeared in my lands. My warriors were hard pressed to fight him off. Now he marches east, headed here. He's wiping out the provinces as he approaches. If we were to pull the warriors out of the provinces that he's in right now, what will become of the Elves who don't know how to defend themselves? What of our ellassens and children?"

"Here, here," several voices chimed in.

I noticed it mostly came from the other lords whose lands Gorion had already passed through. It left me wondering what I would do if Gorion threatened my lands of Annwythel. I didn't keep much of a standing army, just the bare minimum required by King Ethele. Most of my lands were farmland, and I needed every hand I could get out in the fields.

King Ethele raised his hand to silence the buzzing room.

"Order. Order," Jirieth banged his gavel on the table and the room quieted down.

"If you don't agree with this plan, Lord Tulese, then what plan do you have to bring to the table?" King Ethele asked, opening his arms wide, gesturing to everyone.

Lord Tulese squirmed a bit in his chair. I would squirm too if the king challenged me. That's why I was keeping my mouth shut today.

"Perhaps we should march all of our armies out to meet him, rather than sit around until he comes to us." Lord Tulese lifted his chin and met King Ethele's gaze.

"I agree with him."

"I think that's a death wish."

"I think it's all a death wish."

"We should pray to the Mighty One. He saved us once before. He'll save us again."

The murmuring in the room grew louder and louder at Lord Tulese's words.

"Enough!" King Ethele bellowed, flying to his feet, his chair shooting back. He didn't even bother to call upon Jirieth to silence the room, though that was Jirieth's job. "Lord Tulese, I know you're upset at the losses to your tribe because of this monster, but I will not allow you to belittle my plans like that. I am the Chief Tribeless and your king. You will have some respect at this table, or I will not invite you the next time we meet."

Lord Tulese pursed his lips, his nostrils flaring. I'm happy he had found his confidence. We had all heard the horror stories coming from his lands. The way Gorion was razing the Mindarin's villages, beheading and burning Elves as he rampaged through the land. This monster had no respect for Elvish lives and Tulese was right. He needed to be quashed and quickly. But I was hesitant to go with Tulese's plan.

Gathering Elves from all the provinces would be hard enough. Yes, we had the Pathstones, the magical way to transport Elves throughout the land to one place fast. But it all depended on whether Gorion was near a Pathstone in his march to the capital. It was the only way we would be able to quickly gather all the warriors we needed to destroy Gorion and his army.

"Yes, Your Majesty," Lord Tulese said with a slight bow of his head to his sovereign.

King Ethele looked around the table. "Does anyone else have a plan they'd like to voice?"

The meeting droned on, several of the lords bringing forth plans that were shot down by either King Ethele or another lord. Everything voiced would either require too much time, which we didn't have, or too much force, which we also didn't have. We'd all seen the reports. With the current Elves in the army, Gorion outnumbered us ten to one. Trescone was the best fortified city in Karaphyllon. It could withhold a siege with battles on the plains for some time. It seemed our only hope.

"Lord Alec, you've been awfully quiet," King Ethele said, looking over at me where I sat in between Lord Grimwald of the Dumnonia Province and Lord Aleric of the Avar Province. "Everyone else has voiced something. Did you have any plans to bring to this council meeting?"

I looked around the room as all eyes turned on me. Everyone looked grumpy after such a long meeting, and I received several frowns.

"I agree with your plan, Your Majesty," I murmured, the utter silence of the room making me sound almost as if I were shouting, though I nearly spoke in a whisper.

Lord Tulese scoffed, and Lord Rinion's frown deepened. Even Jirieth, the lord who was supposed to be the Speaker and keep order, looked like he wanted to hurl an insult at me.

"It's the only thing that makes sense," I continued, my gaze flicking to the king, then back to the disagreeable lords. "We all know how strong these city walls are. We all know there are only two gates into this city. That means there are only two places Gorion will try to attack us, if he's half the warrior he's made himself out to be. We should go with the king's plan or no plan at all."

I pushed back my chair and crossed my arms, daring anyone to disagree. They all knew what I spoke was true. They all knew what they had to do.

"The lords have all spoken. Let's put it to a vote." Jirieth stepped in and proceeded with the meeting according to his job as Speaker.

We all voted, but few of us were happy about the outcome.

CHAPTER 7
AN ATTEMPT AT BEING CORDIAL

Gwynneth

When I arrived home that evening, Father wasn't there yet. He was still working at the palace. I quickly changed from my soiled work clothes into a tight-bodied gray dress with a flouncing skirt. After washing my face and hands, I went downstairs, where I found Alec sitting in the parlor.

I groaned, dreading having to spend time with him. There was too much pressure on me to fall in love with him. I couldn't bear that eager look in his eyes. All I wanted to do was turn around and retreat to my bedroom, but I knew Father expected me to behave kindly toward our guest, despite all my trepidation about the betrothal decision.

"Hello Gwynneth," he greeted me. Why did he have to smile at me so cordially? "I trust you've had a good day?" He sat on the couch with one leg crossed over the other, his arms outstretched on the couch back, comfortable in our home. He must feel like he knew Father very well.

"I'm doing well, thank you," I answered. I hesitated, trying to figure out where it would be least rude for me to sit. Should I sit beside him on the couch? I couldn't stoop to being that friendly with him, could I? "How was the council meeting today?" I asked, making my decision and taking a seat in a chair across from him. It was a comfortable seat, and still close enough to him to come across as the polite ellassen my father expected me to be.

Father had asked me last night to be more hospitable toward Alec and I'd decided that I would try my best to do so. I hated to disappoint Father, even if he made such poor decisions, like betrothing me off to a complete stranger.

"Ugh, don't remind me about it," Alec said with a groan. "I've never been to a meeting that was such a disaster in my life."

"Oh, I'm sorry. What happened?" I asked, surprised that he thought he knew me well enough to react like this in front of me.

"I'm afraid I can't tell you. All procedures of the council are top secret, and we can't share them with anyone outside of council members. Surely you know that from being the daughter of a lord yourself?" He looked at me with raised eyebrows, expecting me to answer.

"Father tells me very little about his work as a lord, I suppose I'd forgotten that rule." I looked down at my hands, which were neatly folded in my lap, feeling foolish for asking the question.

He smiled at me understandingly. "That's alright. Your father comes across as a very private ellas. I'm not surprised to hear that." He paused, briefly looking down at the dark green carpet before looking at me again. "I wish I could tell you, though. It would help ease my mind."

"I wouldn't tell anyone if you shared the council's secret with me," I said with a conspiratorial smile.

"You're a lot friendlier than you were last night," he said, changing the subject. "Are you feeling better about everything?"

I studied the carpet and bit my lip, unsure of how to respond. "Not really," I replied after a long, awkward pause. I felt his steady gaze on me, waiting to hear my answer, knowing the tips of my ears were turning red. "I'm just putting a brave face on it all," I admitted, glancing up at him.

"Does the idea of marriage scare you that much?" he wondered, his brows knitting together.

The way he looked at me intently, as if he really wanted to hear my honest opinion, made my heart drop into my belly and hammer away like the bell boy ringing the great temple bell in the main square.

"Well, I don't exactly know you very well, now do I?" I answered.

Now it was Alec's turn to bite his lip and look down at his hands.

"How did you hear about me in the first place?" I'd been wondering this all day, just hadn't voiced it to anyone.

"I got to know your father quite well about two years ago. We were working closely together on an extensive project for the country, part of our duties as Lords of the Council. He somehow mentioned you in our conversation, speaking very highly of you, and I suppose that was what piqued my interest in you. We started corresponding a few months after that."

"How often did you correspond with my father?" I asked.

"I think I got a letter from him every two weeks or so. That's about the time a letter takes to travel from Annwythel to here," he answered.

"And when did you tell him in your corresponding that you wanted to be betrothed to me?"

"Um...about six months ago. With every letter, he told me more about you and I found myself falling in love, even though I'd never laid eyes on you."

"And somehow, in all the letters, he never mentioned that I was a blacksmith?" I raised my eyebrows, pointing out the obvious question.

"No, he avoided that topic," he said.

"Funny," I said, getting angry with him and Father all over again. "Because blacksmithing is what I do most of the time. What else did he have to say about me? My job is such a huge part of my life."

"Perhaps he doesn't think so," Alec said innocently.

"No, he doesn't," I said irritably. "Father never wanted me to take on an ellas's trade." I sighed and shook my head, looking down once more.

"Why did he let you take up blacksmithing in the end?" he asked, his voice gentle.

"My brother, Timithen, was to be apprenticed to Master Carlel, and I begged to be allowed to as well. We were best of friends. I did everything Timithen did, even if it got us both in trouble," I said, thinking back to the good old days when we were children.

"And he readily consented, even though he didn't want you to?"

"Timithen, Mother, and I fought him over it for a long time, even bringing it up with Master Carlel. He threatened to not take on Timithen unless he took on me as well."

"Ah, blackmail. I see," Alec said with a grin, leaning forward in his chair.

I looked back up at him, amused to see him eagerly waiting for me to continue my story. "And when Timithen and Mother died, well...Father couldn't bring himself to make me give up my trade," I ended.

"I'm sorry. Timithen must have been very close to you," Alec said with feeling.

"We were twins," I said with a smile. "Inseparable." The conversation paused, memories of Timithen crowding into my head. "You're really in love with me?" I asked suddenly, biting my lip nervously as his words from a moment ago dawned on me.

"Yes," he murmured, keeping his steady gaze on me. "Every minute I spend with you, I like you more and more. You're a very nice ellassen to be around. Now that you're not angry with your father and me anymore, that is." He finished his sentence with another smile.

"Thank you," I said. I couldn't help but smile a little. He was such a pleasant ellas. Why was I opposed to being betrothed to him? "I don't see what makes me an eligible bride for the Lord of Annwythel. There must be other ellassens that you already know that are better than I am."

"There are other ellassens, but they're not better than you," he said with a decided shake of his head.

"You could have a wife who has more connections than our tribe. Father keeps us in Trescone year-round. I've never even been home to the Finthwore province. We...I don't know that many important Elves. You don't desire someone with more power?"

"I desire someone who shares common interests with me."

"And I do?"

"Yes."

"What do we have in common?" I wondered.

Just then, Father walked in, and our rather personal discussion came to an abrupt halt. Father, as always, had a subject to broach, and the conversation took a rather boring turn. I had a hard time paying attention to the ellases talk because Alec's last comment got me thinking. What did he already know about me and how were we similar?

—◦✦◦—

"Any news of how close Gorion and his forces are to reaching the capital?" I asked Father at supper.

It was dark outside, and we were eating by candlelight in the formal dining room. The long table stretched down the center of the room, the three of us all sequestered at one end. Father sat in the chair at the head of the table, and Alec and I sat on opposite sides, staring awkwardly at each other. At least, I felt awkward. Alec looked well at ease, as he always seemed to be in our home.

"I think Alec might be able to tell you more about that, Gwynneth. He sat in on the top secret council meeting today while I did not. King Ethele had me busy elsewhere," Father answered, taking another bite of his soup.

I turned to Alec. Though I still felt a little awkward talking to him, I had to admit this evening before Father came home had been pleasant.

"Well?" I pressed when he said nothing. He was probably still sorting through what he could tell me and what needed to remain confidential. He hadn't wanted to tell me anything earlier in the parlor.

"The enemy gets closer to us each day that passes," he murmured without looking up from his bowl of soup.

"And how many Elf warriors have arrived in the capital so far?" I questioned.

"I can't give exact numbers, but the council just put out the call for all able-bodied warriors to come to Trescone," he said, still not looking up at me.

"I thought that had already happened?" I asked, turning to my father.

"The council has to follow certain procedures, my dear, and having the lords meet as one was the first step in many to take care of this threat to our lands," Father patiently replied.

I turned back to Alec. He had been the one to hear the council's decision today, after all, not Father. "Do you think enough will arrive by the time Gorion gets here?" I asked.

"I'm not sure. I know many will come, but we'll have to make do with the soldiers that we have by the time Gorion arrives on our doorstep," he answered.

"Is something wrong, Alec?" I asked. He hadn't looked up at me during this entire conversation. It wasn't like him.

"I'm just tired, that's all," he answered, glancing up at me. But his eyes were clouded with worry.

I didn't believe him. He said earlier that he wished he could tell me what had happened at the meeting to ease his mind. He had called it the worst disaster he'd ever witnessed. I wondered what he'd meant by that. Obviously, whatever had happened at the meeting today was worrying him immensely, but he couldn't tell anyone about it.

"It's alright if you break their trust, you know," I whispered to him as we were walking back into the parlor.

He gave me such a sad look I thought he might be on the verge of tears.

"What happened today at that meeting?" I asked. The dejected way he was acting worried me, made me fear for the city's safety. I wished I could do something to help him.

"I wish I could say, but I can't," he whispered back, his eyes earnest.

"If we do marry, would you still have to keep secrets from me?" I asked. We had paused in the hallway in between the dining room and the parlor.

"Only if the safety of the world depends on me not saying anything. Otherwise, I'll tell you everything when we're—" he broke off, probably afraid to say the word, for fear that it wouldn't happen. "Are you considering it now?" he asked, a hopeful glint coming into his blue eyes. But he still looked extremely sad.

He meant was I considering marriage, and my heart dropped into my stomach. "Well, I suppose with each hour that I spend with you, I grow more comfortable with the idea," I admitted, attempting a smile, anything to cheer him up.

He reached out and swept his hand down my arm. I pulled back in utter surprise. His light touch sent tingles down my spine.

"I'm sorry. I shouldn't have done that. Forgive me," he said, then hastened into the parlor to join my father, the special moment between us forever gone.

He had been wrong to touch me like that. Fanwases and fanwassens touched each other in their games until they were around ten years old. Then it was considered improper for fanwases and fanwassens and young ellases and ellassens to touch each other until you were either betrothed or married. And then you only touched your spouse. That was just how we did it here.

I stayed in the hall a few more seconds to compose myself before I joined the ellases in the parlor. There was no way I could let on that Alec had just broken the chief rule for proper behavior toward an ellassen. I didn't want to get either of us in trouble, even if it was Alec who had been at fault.

When I joined them in the parlor, they seemed deep in conversation. Something about the population of the Unthwas Tribe.

"So, Gwynneth, how's my sword coming along?" Alec asked when I took my seat beside him on the couch.

"I worked on it a bit today, actually," I answered with a smile. "Hopefully it'll be ready by the battle, but we also have a lot of work to do to finish up the weapons for the incoming warriors. I can't make any guarantees that I'll finish it anytime soon. I'm sorry I told you otherwise when you dropped it off at the smithy. I didn't realize how busy we were with the king's order for swords." My mind flitted to the fact that Master Carlel gave me permission to work later than usual, but I decided it was better not to mention that.

"That's all right. I don't need it until the battle anyway," he said, smiling at me, all signs of his earlier distress gone.

I wondered if he was putting on a brave front for Father's sake. It wasn't every day you interacted with another lord after work hours. And he, being much younger than my father, probably had him on edge. No doubt he wanted to impress Father in more ways than one.

"Are you going to stay in the capital and fight in the war against Gorion?" I asked, excitement at the prospect of the upcoming battle coursing through my veins. I was grateful Father hadn't mentioned anything about fleeing the city. This was our home. I was sure he would stay behind to defend it and keep me safe by his side while doing it.

"Most of the information I know is classified, but here's what I can tell you. If the information we have is correct,

Gorion will be here in about ten days," Alec answered. "The king doesn't want us lords to fight since we're on the council," he said, including Father in his words. "But I want to help our land and I think I can help the most by fighting alongside the other ellases." He paused, eying Father for his assent. My father nodded, an understanding smile on his lips. "Especially since it looks like we won't have as many warriors as we'd hoped for, which spells our doom, I'm sure. But I'd feel like a coward if I escaped back to Annwythel before the battle."

"Oh," I said, a sudden fear for his safety creeping into my heart. I didn't care for him, not yet, but the thought of him fighting in the war, perhaps being wounded, even killed, scared me to death.

"Are you feeling all right, Gwynneth? You've gone pale," Alec said, concern covering his face.

"Yes, I'm fine. Just tired," I lied, telling myself I was being silly fearing for this Annwythel Elf that I had only just met yesterday.

"Perhaps you should go to bed early," he suggested, giving me a sympathetic smile. "You've had a long day, I'm sure."

"No, I'm—" I started to object, but then a sudden wave of weariness washed over me, and I sighed. "Maybe you're right. I think I will head up to my room."

I stood up, feeling a little dizzy, and grabbed the arm of the couch to catch myself. Surely speaking of the coming siege wasn't making me this afraid? Alec stood up, his quick hands grabbing me around the waist and holding my arm that wasn't resting on the couch.

"Come, let's get you into bed," he said. "You're worn out."

I allowed him to half-lead, half-carry me out of the parlor and up the stairs. Father quietly followed us to the bottom of the stairs, his face stern. No doubt he disapproved of Alec helping me in this way. Alec helped me upstairs, opened my bedroom door, and guided me to the bed, to my surprise. I thought he'd follow customs enough to not enter my bedroom, but he must have been very worried about me. This was just exhaustion from a long day at the smithy, not something else. But the way my heart skittered in my chest as Alec eased me onto the bed, I knew it wasn't all weariness from hard labor.

He pulled the bedsheets down and covered me up once I'd laid my head on the pillow. Even more surprising to me, he dared to sit on the edge of the bed and gently tuck me in, his hand caressing my brow as he gazed at me, his blue eyes showing both concern and fascination. He must think I was very beautiful.

"Thank you," I murmured, smiling faintly at him.

"What happened down there?" he asked, still seated on the edge of my bed. All I could think was how improper this was for him to do.

"I don't know exactly," I said, afraid to admit the truth.

"Well, get some rest. I hope you feel better in the morning," he said, getting up to leave.

"You speak lightly of your imminent death," I said when he was in the doorway.

He turned and walked back toward me, a smile on his face.

"So, you're worried about me. Is that it?" he asked, taking a seat on the bed again.

"Well, you're the only ellas who's ever cared about me. I know I'm not going to get married, but...you care about me. Shouldn't that mean that I care what happens to you at least a little?"

He smiled at me, a warm, knowing smile. "Perhaps," he said. "Sweet dreams," he whispered, and was gone.

That night, I dreamed I had known Alec all my life and been in love with him for half of it. In my dream, I accepted his offer of betrothal.

⌖

Alec

I flew back downstairs and paced in the now empty parlor, glad that Lord Cedgewick had retired to his study for the night. I couldn't face him, not after what I'd just done. His look of disapproval made me thankful he wasn't in here upbraiding me for it right now.

I shouldn't have touched her arm in the hallway during that moment when her father wasn't looking. That one slip had led to me helping her to her room when she'd seemed tired and entering her room to tuck her in. Things forbidden by our society. Things her father would surely talk to me about. I shouldn't have done it all, shouldn't have crossed that bridge. I just...I felt so many things for her. And yet she barely knew me.

Barely knew how highly I thought of her.

Barely knew how much I needed her.

I thought the world of her. In his letters, her father described her personality, her amiable qualities, what endeared her to him, and would also endear her to me.

If her father knew the secret me and my family carried with us, he might not have considered this betrothal. But Mother had sworn me to secrecy. If it somehow got out, it would ruin our family.

I needed her in my life. After what had happened to my father, I needed her gentle spirit to bring balance to my life. Needed her ferocity to give me courage to face the lords who opposed me on the council. Needed her beauty to help make me a better person, too.

And she had no idea about all of this. How could I even put it into words?

I stared at the fire until I couldn't keep my eyes open and there was nothing but glowing embers in the fireplace. Then I trudged up to bed with a despairing heart. Would she ever learn to love me back? Or would she refuse my offer?

CHAPTER 8
MY LIFE OF FREEDOM IS OVER

Gwynneth

We were all jerked wide awake in the middle of the night to a loud, persistent knocking on the front door. I jumped out of bed and made it to the front door in time to see Father speaking with a messenger from the palace.

Looking back up the stairs, I saw Alec halfway down them, dressed in black silk bedclothes. I stared at him, open-mouthed, appalled to see him in his nightclothes, and quickly turned my eyes back toward the front door. Fortunately, I had fallen asleep in my day clothes and was at least rushing to the door fully dressed. No need to be embarrassed that way.

"He's severely injured. We're not sure if he'll make it through the night," the messenger was saying to Father. "He's asked to see you. You and your daughter."

Father turned back to look at me and nodded, then turned back to the messenger. I took that as my cue to get dressed. I wondered who we were going to see. What could someone have to tell my father and me that was so important? I pushed past Alec on the stairs up to my room.

"What is it?" he asked, following me up the stairs.

I walked into my room, and he stopped at the threshold, looking for all the world like he wanted to come in, but knew it wasn't allowed.

"Do you mind? I'm trying to get dressed," I said, attempting to close the door.

"You're already dressed," he said, indicating my clothes and putting his hand up to stop the door from shutting. "What is it?" he repeated.

"I don't know. Someone's come for me and Father. I think someone summoned us to go see a dying Elf. I don't know who," I said. "Now please."

This time he let the door close, and I hastened to pull a sweater over my clothes and put on some shoes. When I emerged from my room, I jumped in surprise to find Alec still standing there.

"Can I come with you?" he asked.

"I don't know. You'll have to ask Father," I answered, pushing past him and heading back downstairs.

Father wasn't there, so I assumed he was getting dressed as well. Alec stood there at the top of the stairs, still in his nightclothes, completely unaware of my embarrassment at his state of undress. Two minutes later, Father came downstairs.

"Let's go, Gwynneth. Hurry," he said, ignoring Alec.

"Can I go too, sir?" Alec asked from his position halfway down the staircase.

Father shook his head, took my arm, and we headed out into the night, going toward the palace with the light of the servant's lantern the only thing to light our path on this moonless night.

He led us through a back entrance into the palace and, to my surprise, he didn't head toward where the king and the other nobility slept, but to the servants' quarters. The servant ushered us into a small, poorly lit room toward the end of the hall.

A young ellas lay upon the bed. We could hear his la-bored breathing from where we stood in the doorway, open-mouthed and silent. I had never seen someone's clothes as bedraggled, torn, and bloodied from a fight. Bandages covered his torso and head.

An old ellassen sat on a stool beside the bed, keeping watch over him. Though her face was ageless like us all, I could tell her age by the color of her hair. White. At least a five-hundred-year-old Elf, then.

Father rushed to the ellas's side and knelt by the bed.

"Gimwell, what happened?" he asked.

I wondered who this young Elf was, how he knew Fa-ther, and why he'd asked to speak with me, too.

The Elf turned his head to look at Father, his face filled with pain.

"Cedgewick, I'm glad you came. I had to tell you before I died," he paused, gasping for breath at the effort of speaking.

Clutching his bandaged side, he moaned. The sound of it sent an eerie chill down my back, and I shivered. The nurse rose from her chair and bent over him, checking his wounds. Bloodstains were beginning to seep through the bandages. He looked very young, younger than me.

"Tell me what, Gimwell?" Father said, emotion causing his voice to shake. He must know this Elf well, even though I had never seen him before in my life.

"He's coming, Cedgewick, he's coming," the Elf began. I could hear the terror in his voice, see it in his eyes, even from where I stood at the foot of the bed. "His followers are as numerous as the sand of the sea. Everywhere he goes, all Elves die. There are none who can stand in his way and survive." He clutched Father's shirt and pulled him closer. "I've seen him!" he exclaimed. "This demon from the Black Lands will conquer all of Karaphyllon and leave it a wasteland. All that we know and hold dear will perish. It's futile trying to stand against him."

"But we must make our stand," Father said, easing the ellas's fingers from their grip on his shirt.

"No, you don't understand what I'm trying to say," he said, shaking his head wildly. I noticed his eyes didn't look right, but I couldn't place what made them different from any other Elf's eyes. "Listen to me, Cedgewick. We cannot stand against him." He paused for a breath. "We must join him."

No one in the room moved or even dared to breathe. What treason was this poor servant saying? Gorion had obviously injured him, and he had lost his mind.

"You must listen to me!" he exclaimed when he saw our shocked expressions. "You're close to the king. Speak to him. Convince him to surrender. Gorion will spare all our lives, and though we'll be his servants, we'll at least get to live."

"Did you have anything else to tell us?" Father asked, refusing to agree to the crazed Elf's request.

"The ellassen. I need to speak to the ellassen." He pointed a shaking finger at me.

Father nodded at me, and I stepped up to the young Elf's side.

"You're to play a part in all of this." His whisper was so soft, I could barely hear him. "I don't know what yet, but you will...you will..." he broke off, then turned back to Father. "Lord Cedgewick, please." His eyes were insistent. He must be thinking of his plea for Father to speak to the king.

Father gently pushed me away, placing himself in the Elf's line of sight once more.

"If you will not listen to me, I'll-I'll go..."

His breath was now coming in light, hurried gasps; his voice dropped to the softest of whispers. Father leaned down closer to catch his last words. I saw Gimwell's lips move but couldn't hear anything. Then, the Elf leaned back and breathed his last, his eyes still fixed on my father.

Father jerked back from the dead Elf, shocked at his confession.

"Come on, we're leaving," he said.

He rushed out of the palace, and I had to run after him to keep up. He didn't slow his pace the entire way home and, once inside, he shut the door with such force that it closed with a resounding bang. We stood in the hall in complete darkness.

"Father? What did that Elf tell you?" I asked, concerned.

I glanced up the stairs where Alec sat on the top step, still in his bedclothes. Had he stayed there this whole time?

"Doesn't matter. Go to bed, Gwynneth," he ordered. "You too," he said, a command toward Alec, who stood up and nodded before retreating into his bedroom.

I turned toward the stairs.

"And Gwynneth?" Father said. "Come see me before you go to the blacksmith shop tomorrow."

"Yes, Father," I said, then trudged up the stairs and back to bed.

I fell into my dreams thinking about Gimwell's words to me. I would play a part in this somehow. But how?

The next morning, Father was absent at breakfast, so I stopped by his study on the way out the door to work. He was there, sitting in an armchair staring at the fire, his hands folded together, a somber expression on his face.

"You wanted to see me before I left, Father?" I asked, hoping perhaps he would relay the mysteriousness of last night's encounter with the young Elf on his deathbed.

"Yes, I did," he said, looking up at me. "I want you to stay home today."

"Why?" I asked. He'd never asked me to stay home from work before. I sighed. This was obviously not the conversation where Father would tell me everything Gimwell had whispered to him.

"From now on, your apprenticeship to Carlel is ended. You'll stay home and take on some household duties. Collette will teach you how to cook. I have arranged etiquette classes for you with Princess Selena's old governess. You'll be joining her every afternoon for training."

My heart sank.

Princess Selena was no longer in Karaphyllon. The king had sent her off to another world called Neim when we'd first received tidings of Gorion's arrival. That was years ago, back before he had a name and we just called him the Shadow. King Ethele thought she was the right Elf to go there and relearn the ancient magic for fighting and defense against beings such as Gorion and his Throes. Her being one of the Chief Tribeless's blood, we all believed she was the best candidate for this task and had sent her off with our blessing.

That Father selected me to study with her old governess, as if I hadn't completed my training as an ellassen before Master Carlel had selected me as his apprentice, made me want to spit. I knew I was missing my last year of school, but surely that didn't matter.

"But—" I began. Fury rose in my chest, making it hard to breathe. I was a week away from finishing my apprenticeship. I had worked three long, hard years for this, and now Father was just going to strip it all away? How could he? I wouldn't even get to finish Alec's sword.

"Don't try to persuade me otherwise. I've already made this decision and you will obey me," he said, his face absolute seriousness.

"Yes, Father," I murmured, looking down. My cheeks burned with anger. "Was that all?"

"Yes. You'll spend the morning with Alec. He doesn't have meetings at the palace until this afternoon," he said. "You may go."

I rushed out of the room so Father wouldn't see my hot, incensed tears. How could he end my apprenticeship all of a sudden? What was making him take such drastic measures? I ran into the parlor where Alec was sitting, just opening a book to read. He quickly set it down and stood up, seeing my distraught face.

"Gwynneth? What's wrong?" he asked, concern written all over his face.

"Nothing!" I said, as a sob choked out. "It's nothing. Just leave me alone."

Forget what Father wished right now. I couldn't bear to be in the same room as Alec, not in my distressed state. I turned and rushed out of the room and up the stairs. Hearing him following me, I tried to slam my bedroom door in his face, but he easily stopped it and held it open, even when I pushed against him.

"Gwynneth, tell me what's wrong," he begged.

"No! Go away. I know this is all your fault!" I screamed at him.

"What's my fault?"

"Go away!"

"I won't let you close this door until you tell me what's wrong and why you're crying," he said obstinately.

"He ended my apprenticeship. I hope you're happy!" It came out half a sob, half a shout. "I'm sure he'll also force me to become betrothed to you, and you'll all get your way. So go on. Rejoice. You've won!"

With that, he let me slam the door shut, and I quickly locked it. I sank onto my bed, my body shaking with sobs. My life of freedom was over.

CHAPTER 9

ARRANGEMENTS

Gwynneth

I came out of my room hours later, my stomach growling. Abating my hunger was the only reason for leaving and facing them again. It must be around time for lunch. I hadn't bothered to check the clock on my bedroom wall. I stole down to the kitchen, hoping to avoid them, only to find Alec in there making a tray of food.

"What are you doing here?" I asked, feeling self-conscious about my earlier tirade. "Aren't you supposed to be at a council meeting or something?"

"I sent my apologies to the council this morning. After you didn't spend the morning with me as your father planned, I wanted to make sure you were all right," he said, turning to me and placing both hands on the counter behind him. "Your father told me to let you know you're expected at the palace at a quarter to three."

He pressed his lips together. No sign of his opinion of my father's orders. He turned back to the lunch tray he was making, and an awkward silence filled the room.

"Where's Collette?" I asked after a few minutes, inquiring after our cook.

"I gave her the day off. She'll be back in time to cook supper. I was going to bring you up some lunch, but since you came down…"

"Thank you," I said. "May I help you finish it?"

"Sure," he said, stepping over to make room for me to stand at the kitchen counter with him. He handed me a vegetable knife to finish slicing the tomatoes while he sliced some ham for the sandwiches. "Your father told me the whole story, and I wanted to let you know that none of this is my fault."

"Then whose fault is it?" I asked, needing someone to blame.

"Carlel's," he answered with a shrug, sawing away at the meat.

"What did he do?" I asked, putting the tomatoes on the bread.

"Ask your father," he said. "I don't think it's my place to tell you."

"So, Father told you? How is it I'm always the last person to know anything in this family? You're not even a part of the family yet, and you know everything before me!"

I dropped my knife and stepped back in anger, ashamed that the thought crossed my mind to chase him out of the house with the knife I'd thrown on the counter. Willing it away, I stood there, breathing heavily and staring at him.

"I'm sorry. I can't help it," he said, calmly continuing to slice the meat and place it on the bread. "You admit that one day I'll be a part of the family?" His blue eyes glanced up to meet my stony gaze.

"I didn't say that," I answered quickly, looking down and blushing, wishing to avoid the subject. I stepped back up to the counter and picked up my knife again.

"But you used the word 'yet'," he said, flashing me a quick grin.

"That doesn't mean anything," I objected, refusing to smile. "Now get back to making our lunch."

The sandwiches were soon made, and we sat down at the kitchen table to eat them, not bothering to have our luncheon in the dining room.

"I'm sorry about your apprenticeship being suddenly terminated," he said, taking a bite of his sandwich.

"Me too," I said, downcast.

"I hope you'll enjoy learning how to be a homemaker," he said.

"Why? So, I can become your homemaker?" I retorted. "I'm sorry. That was rude." I looked down. I knew I was upset, but Alec was probably right when he said none of this was his fault. It wouldn't do any good to blame him for everything.

"It's all right," he murmured. I could feel his eyes on me, willing me to look back up at him, but I refused.

That put an end to our friendly conversation, and we ate the rest of the meal in silence. We cleaned up our small mess in the kitchen and went to the parlor.

"Are you going back to the palace when I have to leave for my appointment with Princess Selena's governess?" I asked.

"Probably. The council meetings should still be going on then. I'm happy you're feeling better," he said, taking his usual seat on the couch.

"Not really," I said, sitting in the chair opposite him and giving a sigh. "Just because I quit crying over my father's orders doesn't mean I feel any better about it. Blacksmithing is my life, Alec. I don't know how I'm going to live without it."

"Well, perhaps you won't have to for long," he said.

"What do you mean by that?" I asked. "Is Father going to let me go back to helping Master Carlel?"

"No, but perhaps you could start up your own practice in a different town," he said.

"I haven't finished my apprenticeship. I can do no such thing," I said, then realized that he was getting at something else. "What are you trying to say?" I asked, wary.

"You were right about your father, you know," he continued, not bothering to answer my question. "He doesn't care what you think. He'll have his way with things no matter what you say."

"What do you mean? What are you talking about?" I had a bad feeling in the pit of my stomach at his cryptic words. I didn't like the way this conversation was heading.

"He's arranged everything with the priest," Alec continued, his hesitant gaze meeting mine. "Our betrothal ceremony is in two days from now."

I stared at him, dumbfounded, utterly speechless. I couldn't believe what he was saying. So, I did the only thing that made any sense.

I ran.

Not upstairs to my bedroom. Staying in the house would mean I would have to come back and face him again before our afternoon appointments.

I bolted out the door and down the street.

I didn't know where I was going; I just knew I needed to get away. My tears blinded me, and I stumbled, stubbing my slippered toes. I tripped and fell, scraping my hands and knees. Pulling off my slippers, I flung them as far as I could down the crowded street, hitting a donkey-cart pulled by a silver-haired ellassen.

No one bothered to shout at me. No one here cared.

I crawled to a nearby stable and fell into a pile of hay, shaking with sobs.

A betrothal ceremony?

Two days from now?

My mind went numb, and I couldn't think of anything except Alec's words. *Our betrothal ceremony is in two days from now.* I'd thought that losing my apprenticeship on the cusp of earning my certificate was the end. I was wrong. This was the true end.

⟡

"Gwynneth! Gwynneth!"

I woke hours later to someone in the distance calling my name. It was dark outside. At least I'd managed to miss my first lesson with the princess's governess. Not that I'd been dreading etiquette lessons. I'd taken gobs of them as a fanwassen and had enjoyed them in the past. But at this point, anything that defied my father seemed a win in my book. He was doing his best to destroy any plans I'd made for my life.

I sat up, looking at my torn and dirty dress and my dirt-stained hands. Swallowing hard, I wondered whether I should make myself known to whoever was looking for me, or sneak home and get cleaned up before facing them again.

Opting for the latter, I made my way home, going in through the back gate and sneaking up the servant's stairs to my bedroom. I put on a fresh dress and changed my muddy shoes and stockings. Then I gave my face, neck, and hands a sponge bath, using the cold water in my washbasin by the window. Staring at my red, tired eyes in the small mirror on the wall, I sighed and ran a comb through my long, brown hair, before pinning it into a practical bun, letting the few baby hairs fall in smooth wisps, framing my face. This was the best it would get.

They were out looking for me. I'd best let them know I was home, safe and sound, no matter how much I disliked my father right now and wished Alec would disappear off the face of the earth.

"Gwynneth, where have you been?" Father asked as I entered the parlor, his voice etched with concern.

Lamps lit up the small room. He was the only one here. He stood up and rushed to squeeze my hands as I timidly took a few steps into the room.

"Where's Alec?" I asked. I didn't want to see him right now, but it would be better than facing my father alone.

"He's out with the servants, looking for you." Father sat down on one of the couches, beckoning me to take a seat too.

I slowly sank down on a couch opposite Father, dreading the questioning that was about to come.

"You've been gone for hours, Gwynneth," he began. "We were all worried about you." He sat there, twiddling his thumbs and staring at the carpet.

I had never seen my father look nervous or unsure of himself. Now I faced an Elf who was both those things.

"Alec said he told you about the betrothal ceremony," he began. "You ran away before he could say much."

"There's nothing to say, Father," I said, trying to keep my voice normal, but I heard the hardness etched in it, the hatred I felt for my father. He was the only family I had left. I didn't want to hate him, but he was hurting me immensely. I looked up at him, my jaw set.

His gaze met mine, and I saw the same hardness I felt in his own eyes.

"You will go through with it, Gwynneth," he said with finality.

"I know," I said.

I would obey him. Let him think he'd won. We would be betrothed a year before it came down to a marriage contract. And then I would refuse. Put my foot down once and for all and make my escape. I didn't know where, but I had a year to plan. I could still make something of myself, blacksmith's certificate or no.

Just then, Alec and two ellas servants came bursting into the room.

"There's no sign of her, sir," one servant said, then quieted when he saw me sitting with my father.

"Gwynneth," Alec said, rushing over and taking a seat beside me. "I've been worried sick about you. Where have you been?" He reached out and took my hand, his touch gentle.

If Father wasn't forcing this betrothal on me, perhaps I would have liked his touch. Instead, I pulled my hand from his grasp, right as Father cleared his throat; his silent signal to Alec that he was breaking the rules on proper etiquette between betrothed couples.

"Forgive me, Lord Cedgewick," Alec said, flushing. Then, turning back to me, "Where did you go, Gwynneth? We've been looking for you everywhere. I must say, you're pretty good at hiding." He gave me a sympathetic smile, waiting for me to answer.

Father was also staring at me, waiting for me to speak, tell them my whole story.

"I don't know where I went," I said, looking down at my hands sheepishly. "I'm just glad I found my way home."

It was the truth. I didn't know who's stable I had fallen asleep in, and I wasn't about to tell my father, a Lord of the Council, that his marriageable-aged daughter had fallen asleep in a barn. He would be mortified, maybe even confine me to the house, and I didn't need any more restrictions placed on me. Not now.

"I'm thankful you came home, too, daughter. Safe and unhurt," Father murmured. "It's late. I think we should all try to get some sleep. We have a busy day ahead of us tomorrow. The war still brews, and you, Gwynneth, have lessons with the princess's governess."

My dreams that night were of my upcoming etiquette lessons. Soldiers were teaching me and the governess how to fight so we could hold our own against Gorion's armies, ellassens or no.

⸺◈⸺

Alec

She didn't want me. Her father was forcing her into this, and she didn't want me. I was desperate for her to reciprocate my love. Didn't she know I came to her with an honest heart, wanting nothing but to make her happy? If only she could see inside of it and know these things.

I wanted to give her the world, and she didn't want any of it. I knew it was because her father was forcing her to decide. Forcing her to make the choice he wanted her to make.

He'd made all the arrangements with the priest, then come and told me about it. And since he was Gwynneth's father, he had most of the say in the matter. I just wish he'd given us more time. Given her more time to learn to love me. Given me more time to win her over. Given me more time to tell her my family's secret.

We had kept it hidden for many years. And now that I was trying to choose a wife, she needed to know. I hadn't been able to bring myself to tell Lord Cedgewick. What would he think of us if he knew? Would he back out of this arrangement?

But she trusted me. I could tell her my secret. If only there was a good time to do so.

She'd said she liked me. Was that enough for both of us to be able to go through with her father's wishes? Or would she balk when she heard the truth of my origins of rising as a Lord of the Council at such a young age?

I shook my head. I couldn't let myself wallow in self-doubt anymore.

I needed to give her more. Something that she desired enough that she would want to spend her life with me, the way I wanted to spend every minute of the rest of my life with her.

I just didn't know what.

CHAPTER 10
The Betrothal Ceremony

Gwynneth

It was a day later, the night before the betrothal ceremony, and I was in my room about to get dressed for bed when I heard a soft knock at the door. I opened it to find Alec standing there.

"Yes?" I said, still wary of him.

It had only been a few days since I'd first laid eyes on him and we hadn't talked much in the past day. I'd stayed in my room to avoid the ellases, and they'd both been busy at the palace, preparing for the oncoming siege.

"Can I come in?" he asked.

"Alec, you know it's not proper for you to come into my room. Even if you have done it before," I said.

"Fine, but I need to talk to you," he replied, his expression earnest.

"Alright." I said, folding my arms across my chest as I remained standing in the doorway.

"Are you sure about going through with the ceremony tomorrow?" His blue eyes bored worried holes into me. His lips were slightly parted as he waited for my reply.

"Do you see where I have any choice in the matter?" I asked, lifting my chin. I tried not to make my tone of voice sound as bitter as I felt. He hadn't been the one to push us into this, after all.

"So, you want to marry me in the end?" He placed a hand high on my door frame, leaning in as he asked the question.

"I don't know," I answered with a sigh, warily eying his muscled arm.

I wished Father was giving us time to get to know one another before we jumped into an official betrothal. Wished I'd known Alec for longer. Wished there was something I could do except obey my father. But there was nothing I could do. In our world, Father's rule was law. There was no getting out of this, not for me.

"Is that the best answer you can give me?" he asked. The nervous look in his eyes made my heart sink.

"I'm afraid so," I answered, wishing with all my heart that I could have told him something else, something that he wanted to hear. How could I, though, when I didn't even know him?

"Well, I suppose that'll have to be good enough, then," he said gloomily. "Goodnight, Gwynneth." He turned away to go to his own room, his shoulders slumped. I felt sorry for him, but there was nothing I could do.

I went to bed that night telling myself I was doing the right thing. By agreeing to the betrothal, I'd be pleasing both Father and Alec, even if I still felt divided on the inside. I didn't know what I felt toward Alec. In the past week since we'd met, I'd come to know him a little. He was a likable ellas; probably a very good lord who would make an ellassen a good husband. But the thought of being betrothed to him, marrying him, leaving Trescone for the first time in my life to never return except for a visit, scared me to death.

I didn't know how I could ever truly love Alec like he and Father wanted me to. I'd been focused on a career in blacksmithing for so long, not even bothering to think about ellas and falling in love, that the idea was foreign to me. What did it feel like to be in love, anyway? I had no idea, and there was no one I could talk to about it, either. I missed my mother and her wisdom now more than ever.

I gave a heavy sigh and tried to tell myself I was doing the right thing. But I had a bad feeling that I was getting myself in way over my head with no way out other than to bring disgrace to my family. And with Father being a Tribe Lord, I couldn't do that. He was too important of an Elf to create a scandal. I had no doubt word would reach as far as Finthwore, our home province. So not only would all of Trescone talk about it, but everyone in our tribe would, too.

I fell into my dreams, hoping to find peace and thoughts of Sterathelassa there.

—⊰✦⊱—

Smoke rose from a dark battlefield. Bodies lay all around me. The sun was just rising, casting orange glows on the pools of blood. There was blood everywhere, too much blood. The blood of my people.

I lifted my eyes, and there stood Gorion. His eyes glowed with red flames. Black blood dripped from his gaze, falling onto his beak of a nose and mouth.

He held King Ethele's head in his too-large hand, the lifeless face screwed up in utter agony. Gorion had spared no pain in killing our king. The monster's gaze shifted to look beside me.

Father was there, sword drawn. The hand holding it shaking as he stared Death in the face.

"You shall not pass," Father whispered.

"Yes, you shall not pass," Alec said, stepping up on my other side, blade drawn. At least his hands were steady, his fierce gaze firmly fixed on the monster before us.

Gorion laughed, a terrible croaking noise.

"Oh, little fools," he said. "I have already passed."

He tossed the king's head aside, and with one fell swoop, he severed both Father and Alec's torsos from their legs, laughing all the while. Then he looked right at me. I looked down at the weapon I held in my fist and realized it was no weapon at all. I stood there, facing my greatest enemy, holding a lace handkerchief. That was no protection at all.

⟡

I woke with a start. My heart pounded in my chest and my breaths came in ragged gasps. I rolled over and hugged my pillow to my chest, willing myself to calm down. It had only been a dream. I saw the early morning sun peeping through my curtains, happy to be once more in this realm of reality where I was safe, for now.

I rose and dressed in my betrothal clothes, spending extra time getting ready, making sure I was as presentable as I could make myself. I wanted this to be the best day of my life, even if I wasn't sure I was ready to follow the betrothal all the way through to marriage.

First came my violet bodice over my shift, which was made with the laces in the front, easy for an ellassen to put on by herself. Next, the shorter underskirts, made from a practical white cotton. Then the violet overskirt, a slightly darker shade than my bodice. I pulled on the matching sleeves and tied them in place, then reached for my head-covering.

Though ellassens were usually bare-headed, choosing to wear their hair long and loose, for special occasions, we pulled out the traditional dress and headcoverings of our ancestors from generations ago. Back before the various tribes started dressing differently than the other tribes. Now, we can tell the tribes apart by the way they dress. Before, the Elvish Tribes weren't as distinctive, and they all dressed alike.

The veil was simple and elegant, a matching violet color that I pinned over my hair. The front was short, covering just my face, while the rest trailed down my back and stopped at my calves. I pinned the veil up out of my face for now. I would put it back in place before the ceremony.

After an hour of preparation, I allowed myself to look in the mirror. I looked...stunning. I had only seen ellassens in this traditional get-up at other betrothal ceremonies, weddings, and the few religious ceremonies we Elves celebrated throughout the year, but I had never spent this much time putting on the clothes myself. Now I saw what a difference a few extra minutes made, and I blinked away the tears.

This was supposed to be one of the happiest days of my life. Now, it was stripped to just a formality.

Sighing, I emerged from my room and stole downstairs to breakfast.

Alec was nowhere in sight, as it would have been inappropriate for him to see me before the ceremony. No doubt he had gone to the palace to spend the few hours before the ceremony. Father gave me a warm, welcoming smile when I sat down in my usual spot at the table.

"You look beautiful, Gwynneth. Your mother would be proud of you," he said.

"Thank you, Father," I said, trying to give him a confident smile, but on the inside, I felt like a liar going through with this ceremony Father was forcing me into. I nibbled on some toast but was too nervous to eat much else.

Father had arranged the ceremony for this morning. That way, we had less time to wait. Less time to give me a chance to back out. But I would not back out. I couldn't hurt Father or Alec like that. This is what they both expected of me, and I was going to live up to their expectations and make them both very happy.

If I stopped to think about myself for one moment, I would lose my nerve, back out. And then where we would be?

After an hour of waiting, Father and I walked down to the temple together, hand in hand. Even though I was still indecisive about whether I was doing the right thing, I couldn't help but be a little excited about the whole affair. I was on my way to my betrothal ceremony! Although for years, I'd thought I'd never experience this moment, here I was. And now that I was in the moment, I tried my best to enjoy it at least a bit. If anything, the ceremony would be nice. That was something to look forward to.

The temple was a large building a few blocks away from the palace, made entirely of white stone. Its roof jutted out to make a portico, supported by a row of pillars. Two wooden double doors, stretching from ground to roof, stood in the center of the building. Father opened the door, which was silent on its hinges. I was in awe that this massive door didn't squeak. Inside, there was a small entry hall and glass walls which separated the entrance from the sanctuary.

A warden was standing watch at the glass door leading into the sanctuary, a spear held menacingly in his hands. He lowered it down, blocking our entrance into the main part of the temple.

"Only Elves attending the betrothal ceremony of Gwynneth, daughter of Lord Cedgewick, and Lord Alec, son of Lord Kimmel, may enter," he said in a booming monotone that echoed around the entryway.

"I am Lord Cedgewick, and this is my daughter Gwynneth," Father said.

I kept silent, too startled to speak, but then realized that speaking wasn't necessary.

"You may enter," he said, lifting his spear and stepping aside. Opening the door for us, he saluted Father, fist to chest, as we walked through. No doubt he recognized Father as one of the Lords of the Council.

Though pictures of most Elves were scarce, portraits of the lords spread throughout Karaphyllon were well-known. A lord reigned in his home province for centuries until he decided to move on to Sterathelassa, the Land Beyond the Sea, and left Karaphyllon behind forever.

The sanctuary was so beautiful it took my breath away. It had been ages since I'd been here. The ceiling rose a good twenty feet on the outer sides, sloping upward toward the middle of the building, and reached almost fifty feet high. Two rows of pews lined the sides of the large room, leaving about a five-foot-wide aisle down the middle, which led to the raised dais. Five steps led up to the dais where an altar sat in the middle. Elaborate tapestries hung along the wall of the dais, depicting the Acts of the Mighty One.

The priest attending us today walked back and forth along the dais, waving incense in the air with his censer. His attendants, two young fanwases, lit candles with long wooden candle lighters, moving about the sanctuary, leaving a trail of soft, glowing light in their wake. The priest took no notice of Father and me as we made our way to the bottom of the steps. We stood there for several minutes, waiting.

I was unsure what to do and looked to Father for direction. He merely stood there, hands clasped in front of his long, crimson robes, looking poised and confident. If only I felt that way too. I needed some assurance that I was doing the right thing, going through with this betrothal.

Then Alec arrived.

He was dressed in his richest clothes. Long black pants with white pinstripes down the outer seams. A violet button-down with a matching waistcoat; someone must have told him I was wearing a violet dress. He covered it all with a black jacket with long tails. He looked very much like he was from Annwythel, definitely different from how Father was dressed for the occasion.

Adjusting his cravat nervously, he hurried down the aisle, as if he was eager to get this ceremony started and ended.

He joined us where we stood at the base of the steps leading up to the dais, giving me a friendly smile. His tanned face with those high cheekbones and dark brows was so handsome. His blue eyes shone in the dim lighting. Earnest, honest, gentle.

From the little I'd gotten to know him, I assured myself that I was at least betrothing myself to a good ellas. He would be kind and treat me well. It was more than some ellassens could hope for.

The priest quit his pacing and walked down the steps to greet us, bowing low to all three of us in turn. He wore white robes with blue embroidery in a lotus flower pattern. It flowed all the way to the floor, covering his feet, even when he walked. His head was bare to show openness to the Mighty One. Like all Elves, he was clean-shaven, but bald, the way all priests were required to be.

"Lord Alec, son of Kimmel, and Gwynneth, daughter of Cedgewick, I presume?" he asked, nodding toward each of us when he said our names.

"Yes, Your Worship," Alec replied, using the priest's formal title to address him.

"Come up to the altar. Come, come, come." He beckoned us with an impatient hand, bustling his way up the steps and going around to the far side of the golden altar. His attendants, who had finished their task around the same time as the priest, joined the priest on either side of the altar, standing silently and staring straight ahead.

Alec smiled at me, a warm, comforting smile that I didn't realize I needed. Then the three of us hastened up the steps and faced the priest at the altar.

"No other family here to watch your betrothal?" he asked in a surprised tone, noticing the empty seats below.

"No, Your Worship. Just us," Alec answered.

"Well, let's get started then." The priest pulled an old, leatherbound book from the folds of his robes. He set it on the altar, and it fell open to a passage. The priest began reading the passage aloud in a high-pitched monotone that hurt my ears.

"And the two Elves wishing to be bound by a betrothal must come before the priest in all purity and swear their fealty to each other. The promises they make to each other during the ceremony will be forever binding. To break a betrothal vow is a grievous sin in the sight of the

Mighty One. It will bring dishonor to both households. Therefore, both parties are cautioned that they must be absolutely sure they know the responsibilities required through taking the vow of betrothal, and the dire consequences should the vows not be kept. They must be most certain that this is the course of action they wish to take; to bind themselves to each other, forsaking all other loves, and end the betrothal in holy matrimony."

The priest looked up and stared at both me and Alec with those hard green eyes, all utter seriousness.

"You're sure you wish to proceed?" he asked.

CHAPTER II
The Choice of a Lifetime

Gwynneth

I stood there, feeling my heart beat faster. It was getting hard to breathe. This was it. After I assented, there was no backing out. Not until we decided in a year whether to marry or not.

I swallowed hard and glanced over at Alec, who watched me carefully, looking to my lead for how he would respond to the priest's question.

My eyes shifted to Father, who stood between us, facing the priest. He kept his eyes on the priest, his mouth one long, thin line of determination. He really wanted me to go through with this. I tried not to gasp in shock, because I'd known this coming here today. His lack of empathy made this more difficult.

I turned my gaze back to Alec and gave him the slightest of nods.

I was ready to proceed, come what may.

We turned to the priest and nodded our heads yes.

"A verbal assent is to be heard," the priest said, his voice impatient.

I croaked out a "yes", surprised at how quietly Alec assented as well. Surely, he felt more confident about this than I.

The priest continued. "Who gives this ellassen to be betrothed to this ellas?"

"I, her father, do," Father answered, taking his eyes from the priest to glance down at me. There was no sign of a smile there, no warmth in his eyes. Was he angry at my decision to go through with this because he knew my heart was not in it?

"Very good," the priest said. "And does the ellas have a proper vocation and a home to bring this ellassen into when the time comes that they should wed?"

"Yes, your worship. I am Lord of Annwythel Manor, and Gwynneth shall join me there when we marry in a year," Alec answered.

A year was not a very long time to decide anything, especially a lifelong decision such as a marriage contract. I felt my heart sinking lower and lower as the ceremony continued.

"Very good," the priest said. "And now, if you would join hands over the altar."

Alec placed his hand out for me, and I took it. The priest turned toward a basin of water that was set on a table behind the altar and solemnly poured it over our hands so that the water ran over the altar and spilled down its side.

"This water symbolizes the beginning of your relationship, to be maintained in all purity until the two of you shall wed a year from hence. Lord Alec, do you promise to abide by this?"

"Yes, I do," he answered. His voice carried more confidence in it now, and his eyes never left my face.

"Gwynneth, do you promise to abide by this?"

I looked down at our joined hands, my mouth having gone dry as I realized the finality of this decision. Father had forced it upon me, and there was no way I could object now, not after the priest had poured the holy water on us.

"Yes," I breathed, my lips trembling as I blinked back tears. I was glad my veil covered my face. If Alec could see me now, I'm sure his confidence would fade, too.

"Then by the power invested in me by the Mighty One, I pronounce you, Lord Alec and Gwynneth, officially betrothed."

The priest tightly clasped both our hands for a second in both of his long, slender ones, then let them go.

I quickly withdrew my hand from Alec's grasp and dried it off on my dress, surprised at how short the ceremony had been. The priest turned away and walked out a door in the back of the temple, followed by his attendants. Father led the way back up the aisle and out of the dark building. Alec looked at me with a shy grin as we walked.

"Well, I suppose that makes it official," he said.

"Yes, I suppose it does," I replied, not daring to look at him right now.

I was in a daze. It had happened so quick. Not just this ceremony, but everything. Meeting Alec a week ago, losing my apprenticeship and being assigned other duties, getting betrothed. Now I was officially stuck. I just hoped when the time came for the wedding next year, that I would be ready for it and not withdraw and bring disgrace to us all. Perhaps in this year of betrothal, I'd grow to love Alec. I hoped so. Despite wanting to continue forming my plans for being a single blacksmith, the last thing I wanted to do was hurt him and disgrace both our houses.

I was appreciative he didn't say anything else and left me to my thoughts as we walked. I just hoped that I would get to continue my blacksmithing soon. What wrong could Master Carlel have done to make Father discontinue my apprenticeship with him? Father still hadn't told me, and I was still upset that he had told Alec and not me. Why did he seem to trust Alec more than me? Was it just that whatever Master Carlel had done was so grievous that it would upset me? Or make me see Master Carlel in a bad light? Perhaps I shouldn't even think of him as "master" anymore. I was his apprentice no longer, after all.

We walked down the street together, hand in hand as was tradition, remaining that way till we reached home. His hand was warm and soft. It was large, enveloping mine, and he held on gentle, but firm, as if he was afraid I'd let go.

There was a small feast set on our dining room table that Collette prepared while we were gone. Since it was nearly lunchtime, the ellases fell to it with gusto. My appetite was still gone, and I picked at my plate, putting on a brave front.

I excused myself after the meal to go to my room. I wanted to be alone for a bit. Away from Alec and all the confused emotions I felt toward him.

He knew I didn't like him, but he knew I cared enough about this whole situation not to object at the betrothal ceremony just now. He'd given me these strange looks all throughout our luncheon that made me uncomfortable. I felt guilty, like I was deceiving him.

And I was deceiving him. Both him and Father. I knew it wasn't right, but what else was I supposed to do? They'd both expected me to agree to this betrothal and future marriage, no matter what I wanted to do. Father had forced it upon me, setting the date so soon like he had.

I was just pretending to comply with it. But I felt turmoiled inside. I had to get away from them, at least for a little while. And my bedroom was my closest escape.

I secretly relished the day when Alec would go back to Annwythel. He said he'd only be here in the capital for a week, so he would leave any day now. Somehow, I thought that if he left, my life would return to normal.

I couldn't have been more wrong.

The morning before he left, he had a private conversation with me in the parlor, speaking in a whisper the whole time. Father had just left for the palace after breakfast, and we'd come into the parlor. He startled me by closing the door and locking it as soon as we were in the room.

"I'm not supposed to be telling you this, so you have to promise not to breathe a word of it to anyone else," he started, walking over to where I was standing.

"Alright," I said, a little afraid he was going to break our vows for purity during our betrothal, or something similarly awful, the way he had locked the door.

"The council knows a great deal more about Gorion's movements than I've been letting on, and I'm worried for you, Gwynneth," he said, taking my hand in his.

I instantly pulled it from his grasp, and he continued, brushing over the fact that he'd just broken one of the chief rules of a betrothal.

"He's only about a week's journey away from Trescone by now," he continued. "The reports we have of his rampage through our country are that he's destroying everything in his path to Trescone. They've burned every village to the ground that's on the route here. Every Elf they've caught, they've brutally murdered. Poisoned darts through the brain, burned out eyes, blood everywhere."

I shuddered at the imagery.

He looked down briefly, and a muscle in his jaw twitched. "He seems to have unnatural powers so that he can withstand any weapon used against him. No one has gotten within ten feet of him. His warriors are too many to be numbered. We're calling them Throes. I'm sure you've heard the name. It suits them. They're fierce creatures, like very intelligent animals, very skilled with a sword. But they've proved easier to kill than Gorion himself. In fact, they aren't much trouble to kill at all, as long as you don't have a whole swarm of them attacking you all at once. But all that said, he'll be here in a week's time or less." He looked down at the ground for a second, then back at me, determination in his eyes. "I'm afraid for you, Gwynneth. I'd rather you not be here when he arrives."

"But Alec, I need to stay and help. I know how to handle a sword as well as make them. I know Father doesn't want me helping at the smithy anymore..." Feeling the anger for Father rising in my chest once more, I swallowed it down before continuing. "I'll be alright, I'm sure."

"No," he answered, his eyes never leaving my face. They were filled with concern, and I felt touched that he would care about me so much. "I don't want you to stay here. I've arranged it with your father. You're to come to Annwythel as soon as you can. Unfortunately, you can't come with me today, but your father will make travel plans for you to join me at my home. You'll like it there, Gwynneth," he said, taking my hand again. "My mother and sister are excited to meet you. And you'll be safe. Out of harm's way."

"No, Alec," I said, shaking my head and taking a step back, pulling my hand out of his. "I don't want to come with you. I've never been that far away from home, and Father will need me here. My home is here and here is where I'll stay." I balled my hands into fists. If Alec could be determined, I could be stubborn. "I won't let you take me away. My country is at stake here. I know I can be of use here in the capital."

He gave me a hard look. "You realize now that we're betrothed you must obey me?" he said. It wasn't a question. "I'm ordering you to join me at Annwythel in three days' time," he said, his voice almost as stern as Father's. I wondered where the kind, gentlemanly Elf I knew had gone. "If you disobey me, I'll come back here and take you there myself. I won't see you harmed in a battle that you could have escaped from!" He ended with a shout of such passion that I stepped back, looking down.

I was too angry to meet his eyes. How could he order me around like this? He had no right to tell me what I could or couldn't do. We weren't married yet. My fingernails bit into my palms. The pain felt good.

"Gwynneth, look at me," Alec said, his voice normal once more. Gentle, even.

I slowly looked up and met his eyes, touched by the utmost concern I saw in their blue depths.

"I'm only doing this for your protection," he murmured, no sign of anger or hardness about him any longer. "I'm not trying to lord my authority over you for no reason. I want you safe, dearest. Do you understand?"

I nodded, still too angry to speak. How could he take me away from here and leave Father behind?

"It's about time for me to go," he said. "I'll see you in a few days, then. I love you."

I refused to look at him as he said those words. Those words that I had no idea what they meant as far as we were concerned. How could you love someone you had just met?

He waited a few seconds for me to say goodbye or return his love. When I did nothing, he slowly turned and walked out of the room.

Good riddance, I thought. Was Alec going to turn out as controlling as my father? By the Mighty One, I hoped not. He had been a pleasant ellas, very amiable, this whole time. I prayed he would not turn a corner and become something I didn't need.

CHAPTER 12

FORGING A PLAN

Gwynneth

Alec left the next morning, and life with my father returned to normal. Well, the new normal, at least.

Collette was teaching me how to prepare meals. Every morning, we worked together in the kitchen to make lunch. Father would join us at noon to eat the meal I helped to prepare, always complimenting me. I spent my afternoons at the palace having etiquette classes with the princess's old governess. There was a lot I didn't know about how to be a proper ellassen of the nobility. Obviously, I had missed some important lessons not attending the last year of school and beginning my apprenticeship with Master Carlel instead. I still found it hard to think of him as just Carlel, and not "master". It was so ingrained in me.

Princess Selena's governess had much to teach me, and I left each class feeling inadequate to the position I would hold in a year upon my marriage to Alec. I wished the governess would tell me what news she had of Selena studying magic in Neim. But the old ellassen either didn't know anything or liked to keep secrets.

From everything I'd heard about Gorion, we would need Selena's knowledge of magic for fighting before all was said and done. Yet she was slated to be in Neim for the next year, at least. What would become of us here in Karaphyllon before then? Gorion was moving too quick for comfort.

Father returned to his natural self, speaking to me at mealtimes of small niceties, little tidbits here and there of what the council was planning for the war, as much as he could reveal to me. Comfortable, pleasant talks. He was the father I knew and respected, not some overbearing lord who wanted to see me betrothed and married to a stranger as fast as possible, like he was when Alec had been here.

All was well, except for the threat of Gorion's rampage through our little land that we heard of often. Especially with Father on the council, doing his best to fight against the monster's threat to our world.

One day, as I was walking through the palace on my way home from etiquette lessons, I found myself trailing King Ethele and my father, but I was out of their sight. I could tell they were discussing something urgent from Father's gestures, and they were talking just loud enough that I could hear what was being said.

"There must be something you can do, Your Majesty," Father was saying.

"Well, if there is, I wish I knew what it was," King Ethele replied.

The two ellases turned and paused in the hall, facing each other. I stopped in my tracks, listening just around the corner.

"Our Elves are perishing by the droves as Gorion makes his way toward us," Father said. "We have to take our army and march to meet him where he is. We can't wait for him to come here. He leaves a path of death and ruin in his wake." Father paused, lowering his voice so I could just barely make out his words. "We can't let Gorion murder our countrymen in their beds while we remain here, batting down our hatches and preparing for an assault on the capital's walls."

"Do you have a battle plan, then?" King Ethele asked impatiently.

"We've gathered most of our army here, preparing for battle. Organize half of them into their companies and set them out marching toward Gorion's current position, just like I heard Lord Tulese suggest at the council. Have them engage him out in the open country. If we don't stop him completely, we'll at least be able to cripple his army before they reach our gates."

"I don't know, Cedgewick," King Ethele said.

I peered around the corner and saw Father place a hand on the king's shoulder. "Listen to me, Ethele. You can't just sit by and do nothing while this hellhound overtakes our land. We must act, and we must do it now. You have to listen to me."

"You really think it's a good idea to sacrifice half our army?"

"If it weakens his army by half," Father answered with a shrug. "Do you really want the full force of Gorion's strength in arms to come battling at our front door? They will throw our gates down and rip apart our walls within minutes. When the city wall crumbles, all will be lost. Do you really want that?"

"No..."

"By sending out our armies to meet Gorion in the fields, we'll be ensuring the safety of our people," Father continued, speaking quickly as he laid out his plan. "If we're able to weaken him enough, perhaps he'll stop his warpath here. Maybe we'll be able to avoid a battle in the city."

King Ethele sighed. "You really think your plan will work?" he asked, narrowing his eyes at Father, his forehead creased into a frown.

"I do."

"Alright. I'll send the order out to General Verski this afternoon," King Ethele agreed. "Our warriors will march out to meet Gorion by tomorrow morning. I just hope you're right, Cedgewick. I'll blame you personally if this plan fails us in the end."

"Very good, your Majesty," Father said with a shrug.

The two ellases continued walking down the hall, their conversation turning to different matters. I followed them, since we were headed the same way, keeping far enough behind so they wouldn't see me. I didn't want Father to find out I was eavesdropping on a private conversation between him and the king. No doubt no one was supposed to have overheard them.

I couldn't believe what I had heard. Father had convinced King Ethele to act. Finally. We had been sitting on our hands for weeks now, doing nothing but preparing the city for a siege. I was excited about Father's plan, and delighted the king had agreed to it. Now we would meet Gorion head-on and see what our army was made of.

I made my way through the streets, headed back toward home. Lost too deep in thought to notice where I was going, I was caught off guard when I ran straight into someone.

"Oh, I'm sorry," I said, looking up.

It was Carlel.

"Hello Gwynneth," he said with a polite smile. "I've missed you at the shop."

I stepped back, startled at meeting my old master here on the city streets. Yes, the forge was close by, but I hadn't expected to see him here.

"It wasn't my choice to end my apprenticeship," I said glumly, saying the first thing that came to mind. "I have to do what my father tells me." I looked down, unsure of what else to say. "Do you have any idea why he made me quit working for you? He won't give any reasons."

"I don't know. He came to me furious last week but never said exactly what was wrong. Just said that you wouldn't be coming in anymore. And you know I can't give you a completion certificate until you complete all three years to the date. I don't understand why your father would do this to either of us, because I need help at the shop. I'm very behind."

"Well, I don't know what I can do. I'm supposed to be leaving the city tomorrow anyway. I wish I could help you...but...I think I have to obey my father," I said, giving an apologetic shrug.

"He's making you leave because of the upcoming battle?"

"I think it's Alec, my betrothed, who's making me leave. I'm to join him at his home in Annwythel before Gorion's army attacks."

"I see. And you want to go?"

"No," I said. "I know my duty is here in the city to defend it against Gorion. Escaping to Annwythel before the battle makes me feel like a coward. I know I'm just an ellassen, but I can still help."

"Perhaps we could arrange a way for you to stay here like you want," Carlel said, rubbing his chin in thought. "You could help me in the shop, stay in the room above the forge. Finish your apprenticeship." He gave me a smile. "You wouldn't have to tell your father; he'd never know if he didn't see you about the city. In the meantime, you can be here helping me finish the weapons. And Gorion will be here in a week anyway. By then, it will probably be too late for you to escape."

"You'd do this for me?" I asked, hope rising in my chest. I wanted to be here for the battle, do my part in the fighting. Timithen had taught me everything he knew about sword fighting back when he was taking lessons.

"Yes. I need your help. I'll do anything to get you back. And I want you to complete your apprenticeship, so you'll be able to open your own shop one day." There was a twinkle in his eye, and I couldn't help but smile at that dream. Perhaps it would still come true.

"You don't think Father will find me before Gorion reaches the city?" To finish my apprenticeship would mean the world to me. But I knew Father would put a stop to it the moment he found out.

"No, he doesn't come near the shop when he's here at the palace and he never comes to my house. He has no need to speak to an old blacksmith. Your whereabouts will be unknown, I promise."

"Alright," I agreed. "So, I order the carriage to drop me off somewhere outside the city, then make my way back in?"

"You should try to cancel your travel arrangements by carriage and walk to the coach station. Then you can just walk to the forge instead."

"I can try," I said.

"Anyway, I need to get back to the shop," he said, glancing in the direction of his beloved smithy. "I'll see you tomorrow then." With a wave, he walked off.

I headed home and repacked my bags. I had previously packed them with proper attire for staying at a lord's house with all my best dresses. Now, I kept one good dress and packed all my old work clothes, trembling in anticipation of deceiving my father and hiding out in the city with Carlel to finish my apprenticeship. I'd never done anything this rebellious. At least, not since Timithen died. But Father had never been as demanding as he was now, asking me to give up my hopes and dreams, all for the hope of a marriage in the end.

I felt a stab of guilt standing there, staring at my repacked bags. I'd be disappointing Father and Alec by staying here and returning to work at Carlel's. But he needed my help from what he'd told me just now in the street. Father and Alec would be worried sick if I didn't show up at Annwythel four days from now. And I'd miss meeting Alec's family. From what he'd told me of them, I knew I'd like them.

I hardened my heart and pushed away these reasons for obeying the ellases in my life. The city needed my help. I was a blacksmith of the city, in charge of producing the weapons we would use to fight this enemy on our doorstep. They couldn't easily replace me, and I would stay here and do my duty. I had to stay behind and help fight our enemies, no matter what anyone else thought.

I closed my bags and waited for the morning.

CHAPTER 13
BACK TO BLACKSMITHING

Gwynneth

I was able to convince Father the next morning that I could walk to the coach station instead of ride in a carriage. I made the excuse that I needed the fresh air, reminding my father of the long ride in a coach with the windows up.

"I suppose," he finally agreed.

Satisfaction warmed me right down to my toes. My plan was working so far.

After an early breakfast, I left Father on our doorstep, waving my goodbye.

"Safe journey!" he called after me.

Why did that make me feel so guilty?

I continued toward the coach station until he could no longer see me. Then I made my way up side streets, heading toward Carlel's smithy.

Carlel was already at the forge, though it was still early. No doubt he'd had to start coming in earlier when I was no longer there to get things started in the mornings. But now I was back.

He seemed as excited about this whole adventure as I was, showing me up to the little attic room above the smithy, talking eagerly the whole time. We had to walk outside the blacksmith shop to get to it, as the stairs were on the outside of the building.

It was dark in the small attic room, except for the bit of daylight that broke through the curtains in the old, dusty window on the far wall. Carlel moved over to the window and pulled the curtain back.

It was small but would work for a home, for a few weeks at least. A bed stood in the far corner, right next to the window. Old wooden boxes and other miscellaneous junk filled the rest of the space.

"I'm sorry it's so cluttered," Carlel apologized. "I've been using this for storage for several years and haven't had the time to go through and get rid of anything."

"That's all right," I said. "It's not like I'll be living here forever."

"Feel free to move anything if it's in the way. And if you see something you'd like to use, help yourself."

"Thank you, Master Carlel," I said. It felt good to use the proper term for an apprentice to her master, rather than just using his first name, like all the other Elves did.

He left me to get settled, and I quickly changed into my work clothes and hurried down the steps to join him at work.

My heart raced with excitement about returning to blacksmithing. The possibility of graduating from my apprenticeship and being able to open a forge of my own one day was forefront in my mind. I would see this through.

Master Carlel was already deep in work at the shop, and I greeted him and got to work alongside him. Soon I was sweating profusely from the heat of the fire and my shoulders ached from the effort of pounding away at the metal we were shaping into weapons. It felt good to be dirty and sore like this again. I had missed the hard work and the pride I took in it, even though it was only a little over a week since I'd left.

I wondered how long it would take before Alec and Father missed me. It was a three-day journey by coach to Annwythel, it being one of the nearest provinces to Trescone. So, I had at least three days of freedom before Alec would miss me and they would begin searching for me.

By then Gorion's forces would be closer to the capital, perhaps too close to escape to Annwythel like a frightened ninny, as Alec and Father wanted me to. I gave thanks to the Mighty One for that. Not that I didn't want to go to Annwythel. I did want to visit it at least once before I went to live there. But it was the fact that Father and Alec were making me go there to escape the war here. This was my home as much as it was Father's and King Ethele's, and I would stay here to help defend it.

In the meantime, Carlel desperately needed my help if he was going to finish making all the weapons in time. We had already given everything that we had made to the soldiers here in the city. They would need more weapons, and it would take both of us working all day to finish making them, even with our magic.

"Did you hear about the company of warriors that left the city this morning to go meet Gorion in battle?" I asked Master Carlel, wondering if any of the citizens knew.

"No, I haven't heard about that. There seemed to be a lot of hustle and bustle about the streets earlier than usual this morning, though," he said. "I was wondering what all the commotion was about. How did you hear about it?"

"I overheard Father and King Ethele talking in the palace halls yesterday," I said, a little afraid of what Master Carlel would think of me for eavesdropping.

"You're a fortunate one, being the daughter of a counselor to the king. You must hear of a lot of things the king commands before the rest of us do," he said.

"Not usually. Father tells me a few things, but only if they're important to know for my safety," I said. "What are you going to do when Gorion reaches the city? Surely, you're too old to wield a sword and help fight?"

"Do I look that old to you?" he asked, turning his silver head toward me.

Like all Elves, no age lines showed on his face. It was ageless, beautiful. I realized I didn't know how old Master Carlel was. All I knew was that he had a family. Grown children who had left Trescone one by one to find their way in the world. And his hair was silver, not white. He wasn't as ancient as some Elves that still walked in Kara-phyllon.

"I'll have you know these bones of mine still have plenty of strength left in them," he said. "I intend to draw my sword alongside all the other warriors and defend our city with them. What about you? Did your father train you how to handle a sword?"

"Father didn't. He never would have allowed it. But when Timithen was taking sword fighting lessons, he taught me everything he learned. I'm proud to be able to say that I know how to wield a sword, ellassen though I may be," I said.

"That will come in handy with the looming battle. No doubt you'll play a vital part in defending our city," he said.

"Why do you think that?" I asked, curious about his words.

"Just a feeling," he answered.

"I see," I said, nodding my head, thinking back to the servant Gimwell's words as well. *You're to play a part in all of this.*

Our conversation ended, and we worked in silence for a while. Master Carlel's statement got me wondering. What part did I have to play in this war against Gorion? Even though I had heard a lot about Gorion, more than most Elves with Father being on the council, I still didn't know that much about him or his purpose here in Karaphyllon. Everything I'd heard about him made him seem like some sort of invincible creature of Dark Powers. How he had come here, I didn't know. But he was here now, and we had to deal with the threat he brought to our land. So far, every Elf that crossed his path had perished at his hand or at the hands of his followers. Why were they intent on killing us all off? Was there no one who could stop him?

Perhaps there was someone who could stop him. What sort of Elf would that be though? A warrior? Or just a normal Elf with no special skills, like myself? Would the champion of Karaphyllon be a strong ellas, or an ellassen? How would we ever be able to find out who could defeat Gorion, or if anyone could? Did the presence of Gorion spell our doom? Perhaps the end of the world? Is this the way the Mighty One intended our world to end?

So many questions and no solid answers. If only I could find the answers to these questions. I sighed in frustration as I shaped the sword I made. I suppose I'd never get any explanations. Gorion would remain a mystery. We'd only ever know him the way Father had called him: a hellhound from the Black Lands.

I just hoped that I wouldn't have to fight him in the battle. Everyone who had engaged him in combat so far had died horrible deaths. The stories Alec had heard from Elves who had seen him—just seen him, not fought him—were horrendous. *Poisoned darts through the brain, burned out eyes, blood everywhere.* These were just a few of the ways I'd heard he'd killed Elves. Then there was that awful nightmare I'd had about him last week. I shook my head at the pictures etched into my mind through my dreams. How could a creature be so evil?

Perhaps Gorion wasn't just evil. Perhaps he was the source of all evil. Perhaps he was the Lord of the Black Lands. We had heard that a Lord of the Black Lands existed. He was a great Elf Prince once. He was one of the first Elves that the Mighty One created at the beginning of the world. But he had disagreed with the Mighty One's ways. He had wanted to become a ruler over the Mighty One. And so, the Mighty One cursed him. He created the Black Lands, a place of eternal punishment and darkness, for the Mighty Elf who defied His authority, to be banished to for all time.

Maybe Gorion was this Elf, the Lord of the Black Lands. That would explain his great power over all of us. His utter strength and cruelty and why he wanted to kill us. He hated us because we had something that he could never have, a place in Sterathelassa prepared for him.

That doesn't make sense, I thought as I plunged the sword into the quench tank. It hissed as it cooled in the liquid. The Mighty Elf banished to the Black Lands had been just that: banished to the Black Lands with no way of returning here to Karaphyllon, the Living Land.

But it was many thousands of years since that had happened. Perhaps the Lord of the Black Lands had figured out a way to escape his prison in that time. I wished there was an Elf who had answers to my questions about Gorion.

I took the blade out of the quench tank and set it aside. It would need to rest a minute before I could temper it. I took up the next piece of steel to be shaped into a sword.

"Are you sure we can't put any marks on these?" I asked Master Carlel.

"I'm afraid we don't have time for that sort of magic," Master Carlel said, shaking his head sadly. "Just the magic to make the flames hotter and speed up the heating and cooling of the metal as we shape it." He didn't look up as he spoke, his hands never ceased moving. He really was making swords as fast as he could.

"Is the fletcher doing the same thing we are? Using magic for speed rather than art?" It was such a shame that we couldn't enjoy this process. I'd never made this many swords in as little time before.

Master Carlel nodded. "Every weapons-smith is doing the same as us. The order came down from King Ethele himself, not just the council."

"Hmm," I murmured, frowning at the piece of steel in my hands as I flung it into the flames and spoke the spell to speed up the process.

Taking it out of the flame, I beat at the sword with a sudden ferocity, pounding out my frustrations. My eight-pound hammer was heavy, but I barely felt its weight in my arms; I was so lost in my own thoughts.

I hated all these unanswered questions and this threat of Gorion that hung over our heads. All this waiting for our impending doom was driving me mad. I wanted to do something now. Not wait for the monster to lay siege to our capital. What would happen to our land if Gorion won the battle, overtook the capital?

Life as I knew it would cease to exist.

Yes, Father's plans had interrupted my life this past fortnight. But a world under Gorion's rule was so different from Father forcing me into a betrothal. In a week's time, my life as a free Elf of Karaphyllon would probably change forever.

CHAPTER 14

WORRIED

Gwynneth

We worked in silence for the rest of the day. Sometimes the occasional conversation would spark up, only to die a few minutes later. The thought of Gorion's fast approach brooded heavily on our minds.

At the end of the workday, Master Carlel left me in my little attic room above the shop.

"My maid will bring you supper in about an hour," he said, turning to go. "Goodnight, Gwynneth."

"Goodnight."

The old Elf left, and I was alone in my new home. There were no sheets on the bed, so I set about digging through boxes and drawers of furniture in the room, looking for bedsheets and blankets. There were so many things in this storage room, it was like Master Carlel had moved an entire house's belongings in here for storage once upon a time.

I quickly found what I needed and dressed the bed. Then cleared off an old table in the opposite corner. It was a little rickety. The legs weren't all the same size, but it would do for my meals. I moved a few of the boxes around to clear a little more floor space, soon pleased with how my new home looked. All I had left to do was wait for my meal to arrive.

I only waited a few minutes before I heard a soft rap on the door and hastened to open it.

"Hello, miss, I've brought you some supper," Carlel's maid said with a smile.

She was a young ellassen, not much older than sixteen, dressed smartly for a maid.

"Do you want to come in?"

"Oh, no thank you. I need to rush back home. Carlel needs me," she said, handing me the basket of food and turning around just as quickly to leave.

"Goodnight," I called after her.

I closed and bolted the door for the night. It was completely dark outside now. I brought the basket over to my table, pulled up a box for a chair and looked to see what the maid had brought me. It looked like an excellent meal, for being a kind of picnic supper. Warm bread and fresh cheese with an apple. She'd also thought to bring a few things for me to start my own pantry. Some fresh vegetables that would be just as good to eat raw as cooked, a whole loaf of bread, some dried meat, and some fruit. I felt like a queen. Master Carlel was very good to me.

I wondered yet again why father had broken off my apprenticeship with him, thankful once more that I had happened upon Master Carlel on my way home yesterday and he'd come up with this wild plan. I just hoped it lasted long enough for me to finish my apprenticeship. I had only a week left before I would get my certificate and be able to open my own smithy. Alec had mentioned my opening a forge in Annwythel when we married in a year, but I wondered if I could wait that long to open my own forge.

Would I be ready to marry him within a year? Surely, we would see each other more before then and I would get to know him better. Then perhaps I would feel more comfortable marrying him.

Perhaps I would even fall in love with him before our wedding. I still didn't really know what being in love with someone felt like, but maybe I would learn before too long. I should consider myself fortunate being betrothed to such an eligible and handsome ellas.

What was wrong with me that I felt discouraged at the prospect of marrying him? It was probably just the fact that by marrying Alec, my chances at becoming a master blacksmith were slimmer. I'd been thinking about going into this career for three years now and my father forcing me to be betrothed to Alec made me consider other possibilities of a way to spend the rest of my life, and I was not sure that I liked those other possibilities.

I told myself not to worry about the upcoming expectant marriage as I munched on my bread and cheese, sitting at my little makeshift table. If I had not decided about Alec by the end of the year, I could always break off the betrothal. I knew that would mean disgrace for Father, myself, Alec, and his family. But if I truly did not love him and did not want to live with him, I would not continue to lie to everyone and marry him anyway.

Marriage is nothing without love as a foundation. The last thing I wanted was for either of us to be unhappy. I would just have to wait and see how I felt about it in a year. And plan a means of escape from this impending marriage that wouldn't mean disgracing both our families. For now, I would live here and continue to work for Master Carlel. Until Father or Alec found me, that is.

Most likely, Gorion would attack our city, conquer it, and put our people into bondage as his slaves for the rest of our lives before they found me. Then there would be no marriage between Alec and me, and all these petty worries about my future would all be in vain.

I cleaned up my supper and went to bed.

The next day at the smithy was much like the day before. I ate a small breakfast and went downstairs to the shop to start up the fires and get started on our tasks. We had just a few more days to finish up the order of swords for the army, and we had to get it done. We probably only had enough time to finish fifty more swords, which would nearly get us to our quota for what the king had ordered. Without the use of our magic to speed up the sword making process, it would have been impossible to fulfill the order. Once again, I thanked the Mighty One for giving us this powerful magic to use in creating beautiful things. We had to make every moment of every day count if we were going to finish on time.

I wondered what the king would do if we didn't fulfill his order before Gorion attacked us. Fortunately, we had an advanced warning of his approach. It had given us time to call our warriors to the capital, get them sorted and supplied and ready to fight.

I found it funny that hardly any ellassens and fanwases had left the city. Did they not think that the threat of an attack on our city was that great? I thought that they perhaps put too much faith in our city's defenses. We were a well-fortified city, with the high stone walls that surrounded us. But the threat of Gorion's siege was the greatest we had faced in recent history, perhaps in the history of the entire world. You would think that we Elves would take more caution and flee the city.

I was one to talk. My father and Alec wanted me to flee the city, but like the obstinate fool of an ellassen that I was, I had disobeyed their orders and not fled like they wanted me to. Rather, I was hiding out here, of all places. Was I a fool? Only time would tell.

I still wanted so much to defend my city alongside the other skilled warriors, ellassen though I may be.

"Is there any way you can get word from my father, whether he hears from Alec when I don't arrive at Annwythel?" I asked Master Carlel when there was a slight pause in our work.

"I doubt a letter from Alec will arrive before the battle. Gorion is only a few days' march away, and you know how slow the mail is," Carlel said, testing the weight of his hammer in his hand before going back to shaping the crossguard he grasped. "Especially a letter coming all the way from Annwythel. I doubt your father will miss you before the battle begins. But I will try to send someone other than myself to your father's to inquire about you, if it will make you feel better. I know he will not want to see me."

"You still don't know why he's so angry with you?" I asked.

He shook his head sadly. "I'm beginning to wonder if someone spread a lie about me to your father. Even though I get along with most Elves nowadays, I still have some enemies from my past set on destroying me."

I plunged my sword into the quench tank, and it hissed and whined as it cooled, sending steam into my face. Who would want to destroy my master? He worked so hard and kept to his own business. I couldn't imagine how Carlel had managed to make some enemies.

"What sort of lies would break Father's trust in you?" I asked, unsure whether I should press him with all my direct questions. The last thing I wanted to do was cause Master Carlel to clam up, and I needed to know more.

"I don't know," he answered. "All I can make are wild guesses." He tapped more lightly on the sword as he worked his way toward the point. "When do you want me to send a spy to your father's?"

"Perhaps in a day or two," I said, moving on to a second sword that was waiting in the pile of half-made weapons in the corner. "It's supposed to take me three days to reach Annwythel. By tomorrow, Alec will miss me and either send word to Father or come here himself," I said.

"Alright," he said with a curt nod.

I felt a little better with that arranged, but it still didn't mean that I could go very many places in the capital. So many people knew my face, especially near the smithy and the roads leading home. A lot of them didn't know I was supposed to be gone, but if they saw me, they might mention that they saw me to Father. So, if I went anywhere, it had to be somewhere where no one knew me, which was the far side of the capital, near the city's gates. And that was a rather long walk just to buy some food. It also risked the chance of Father seeing me in the streets. All in all, I was pretty much confined to the blacksmith shop and the small apartment above it.

I was at least thrilled to be away from those etiquette lessons. The princess's governess was so strict and boring. She gave all her lessons in a monotone, and I didn't think I'd learned anything the few days I took lessons from her. I don't know how the princess had managed years of this kind of training. But perhaps her current governess hadn't always taught her.

I just wished Princess Selena had been with me for the lessons. It would have made it easier. But she was away on Neim, learning the magic we so desperately needed to know. We lost so much since the Ancient Days, which we needed to regain, especially now with the threat of Gorion.

I missed Father, but I tried not to think about him very much. It made me sad to think how angry and disappointed he would be if he found out how I had disobeyed and defied him. But I had made this decision, and I would not change my mind. Father had been wrong to force my betrothal to Alec. They were both wrong to send me away at our city's greatest need. I could be of help to my city. I knew I could. I was good with a blade, and the Mighty One knows we would have need of every able-bodied swordsman in Trescone.

Gorion's army would be here in four days, from the reports Master Carlel heard in the streets. With each hour that passed, my chances of being able to leave the city and escape to safety grew slimmer and slimmer. I smiled at that. At least I would not end up feeling like a coward being forced by Father and Alec to leave the city.

I was good with a sword; Timithen had told me that. Of course, that had been three years ago, and I had barely touched a sword since then, other than the ones I helped forge. I wondered if my skills with a blade would be rusty, or if my muscles would remember what they had learned so long ago and I would be a deadly fighter. In four days, I would find out, for I would fight alongside the ellases.

⚜

Alec

I paced up and down the front hallway at Annwythel. Gwynneth was supposed to have arrived by now. Her father had told me the day he'd planned for her to leave Trescone, which would have had her arriving last night.

I had stayed up all night waiting for her, pacing in the hallway and wringing my hands. Now I sat in a chair along the hall wall, my head in my hands.

What had happened to her? If only there was some way of knowing.

Images of the worst-case scenarios flashed through my mind. A coach wrecked on the road, Gwynneth trapped inside, unable to get out. The coach somehow getting lost on the roads to Annwythel. And the worst one, her coach attacked by Throes, everyone dead on the cold, blood-stained ground.

I shook my head, willing the images away. I wouldn't let myself think like that.

"Alec, are you still up?" It was Mother on the stairs, coming down for the day. For the first time, I noticed the sun's rays coming in through the window over the front door.

I looked up at her, feeling hopeless.

"She didn't come?" Mother asked.

I shook my head, too tired and worried to form words.

Mother pursed her lips, concern in her eyes as well. "Well, at least come into the breakfast room and have some tea with me, son." She walked over to me and placed a comforting hand on my shoulder.

I stood up, beginning to pace again. "I can't, Mother. I-I need to do something. Anything. I can't just sit down and enjoy a cup of tea. Not when I don't know where she is in the world right now." I squeezed her hand, then headed out to the stables.

Half an hour later I was atop my gelding, Caspian, headed back toward Trescone. I had to get answers somehow.

CHAPTER 15

Thinking the Worst

Gwynneth

Three days later, Master Carlel came into work grinning. It had been a long while since I'd seen him so happy. I knew he must have good news.

"What is it?" I asked, my eyes alight with anticipation from where I stood by the bellows.

"I have news from your father," he said. Then stopped talking and began to work, a secretive smile still plastered on his face.

"And?" I pressed, as I reached out with my magic toward the bellows, commanding them to move on their own accord.

"Alec is back in town," he said. "He's staying with your father."

"I see," I said, looking back down at my work. The bellows were moving nicely, and from the heat of the fire, I could tell it was the right temperature now. I thrust the long, straight piece of dark steel into the fire and cast another spell to make it heat up faster.

I realized that Master Carlel was staring at me, watching me work, knowing he was waiting for my reaction to his news. I didn't know what to think. Alec had come back so fast. It must mean they were both really worried about me.

"Are you going to go see them?" he asked.

"And have them send me out of the city the day before the enemy arrives? No thanks," I hastily said. I felt bad for them, but not bad enough to reveal my whereabouts and miss the chance to defend my city alongside all the other great warriors. This was my one chance to prove to the world what an ellassen could do. Because no one else was going to do it.

"I thought you would have wanted to let them know that you're safe and sound before the battle," Master Carlel murmured, casting the metal piece he was working on into the hottest part of the fire.

"Well..." I reconsidered. Master Carlel had a point. "I'd like to do that, but I can't risk them sending me away. I want to see the battle, help fight, and defeat Gorion myself."

Master Carlel bit his lip. I couldn't tell from his neutral expression what he thought about my statement. "It's probably too late for them to send you away, anyway. Gorion's army is so close that the surrounding countryside is not safe anymore," he said matter-of-factly, looking up to meet my eyes, his gaze serious. "It would be more dangerous for them to make you leave than to let you stay."

"All the same, I'm not going to take my chances. I'll go see them after the battle begins."

"Do what you wish," Master Carlel said. "But I think both of them would be relieved if they saw you were safe and sound before the battle begins. From what my spy told me, they both seemed beside themselves with worry about you."

I smiled to myself. "They have no idea where I am?" I asked. "You would have thought the first place they'd look would be here. Where else would I go to hide?"

"I'm afraid the thought that you're just hiding hasn't even entered their minds," Master Carlel said, his voice grave. "They think the worst has happened to you." His expression was stern, a master scolding his apprentice. "They think Throes attacked you on the road to Annwythel and you are dead."

I gasped in surprise, my mouth falling open in shock. I wasn't expecting them to think something so drastic had happened to me. But these days, our country was not safe, even for small parties to travel across. Gorion's minions, the Throes, were everywhere, like too many ants to all fit inside their nest of an army. Just crawling about, seeking to harm all living things.

I felt sorry for Father and Alec at my home, thinking the worst. It flickered across my mind to go see them, to let them know I was alive. But my heart hardened back into its steely resolve. No, I would let them suffer a few days more. I had to be here in the city to help fight in the war against Gorion.

I couldn't let either of them inhibit my chances to draw arms with our mightiest warriors and defend our land. It was my right to do so if I wanted to, even if I was an ellassen. I was just as capable of killing a Throe as any ellas was, and I would prove it to them.

⬥

It was the day Gorion's army was supposed to reach the city. King Ethele had sent out half our warriors to meet him in the countryside to weaken the enemy's army with a surprise attack. We hadn't heard from those warriors since they left the city. It had been over a week since they'd marched on Gorion. No doubt our foe turned out to be more deadly than the king anticipated, and there were no survivors from that battle. My father's advice to the king gone awry.

Now our army was that much weaker. We would only be able to hold the city for half as long. Perhaps it would have been better if we had just waited for Gorion to arrive at our gates instead of meeting him halfway. I was angry that my father had given such poor council. I thought he was smarter than that, and I felt disappointed to see that he was not.

Master Carlel and I finished making the swords for the warriors that remained to defend our city, and I delivered them to the troops. I set off in a small cart laden down with the weapons and made my way to the gates of the city where the Elf warriors were forming their ranks, and delivered the swords. The soldiers met me a few blocks away from the city walls, among the houses and shops. They smiled their thanks, grateful to receive the swords.

After delivering the swords, I drove my cart a few blocks away from the soldiers, who I knew were watching me and would stop me if I tried to come closer to the city walls. They just saw me as a weak ellassen, someone who would hinder them more than would help them. Once I was out of their sight, I left my cart and began walking toward the wall. I wanted to see the enemy for myself.

When I was nearly at the wall, I saw a group of ellassens running toward me, screaming in pure terror.

"He's coming! He's coming!" they cried, sprinting back to their houses where they hoped to find safety and shelter. They tried to get me to follow, but like the fool I was, I continued running in the direction of the city gates.

I just wanted to get a look at him. Was he really the great formidable creature that everyone said he was? Did he really have the power to scare someone to death just by looking upon his face?

I made it to the wall and sprinted up the stairs that led to the top. It didn't help anything that there were seemingly hundreds of Elves running down the wide stairs at the same time. I fought my way through the crowd, making slow progress. Then I was at the top of the stairs and pushing my way toward the battlements. I had to see this great army that was such a threat to our way of life. Had to see for myself that it was real.

The sight of the army took my breath away. A lump of pure fear popped into my throat, and I tried in vain to swallow it down. The stories were true. He was formidable, and so was his army. All along the ground in front of the city, stretching far into the distance, their vast army marched toward our gates.

The creatures that made up Gorion's army were unlike any I had ever seen before. I couldn't make out what they were because they were still some distance away, but they were not Elves. The creatures had long arms that carried cruel looking weapons. Short, stubby legs covered in some type of fur carried them too fast across our plains. And of course, they were wearing what looked like fairly good, sturdy armor; something metal that an arrow would not pierce, nor would a sword be able to hack through easily. From this distance, I couldn't tell what type of metal it was, but the way it glinted blue in the sun, I thought perhaps it was a new kind of metal, something unknown to our world.

There was no way we could stand against something so threatening. They had huge bridges and carts on wheels. Tall ladders and poles, too. All for the sake of climbing our battlements and attacking us.

Leading the army was Gorion himself. The monster looked like he was from the Black Lands. Hardly any armor covered his purplish flesh. The skin looked rough and scaly. I was sure his very skin was armor of some twisted, evil sort. His hands were claws that looked used to tearing things apart, like us Elves.

The scariest part about him was his face. His horrible, horrible face. The enormous head was at least three times the size of an Elven head. He had two green horns that rose at least a foot from his head and no ears, as far as I could tell. His nose crooked into a beak that looked well-practiced at pecking out Elf hearts.

But the eyes. Even from this distance of several hundred feet away, we all could see those formidable, haunting eyes. One look at them and I was sure I would never be able to sleep without nightmares again. They burned with a red flame, covered in bloodlust.

I found myself looking down after just one glance at him. One glance was enough to burn his image into my mind forever. I would never unsee that monstrous, other-worldly, evil face.

This was a creature no one could stand against, no matter how strong they were.

And he was here.

At our gates.

Ready to conquer our capital and take complete control of our little world.

What startled me the most was that this Gorion looked exactly how I had pictured him in my nightmare a few days ago. How had I dreamed something so accurate?

My hands shook and my knees felt weak as I stood there, dumbly watching the army approach. The other Elves, all ellases, standing beside me on the battlements, must have felt the same way. We all just stood there, mouths agape, staring out into the field. The battle was closing in on us fast. Too fast. There was no fleeing the city now.

I felt like such a fool for not having escaped from the capital when I had the chance. If I had known how large this army was, how indestructible they looked, I would have fled and been pleased to go to Annwythel. At least it was safe there. But now, here I stood, looking certain death in the eye.

I don't know how long we all stood there on the battlements doing nothing. The army got closer and closer to our gates.

I saw now that besides having siege towers and ladders for climbing our walls, they also had a huge battering ram with them. It was being pushed on a massive siege cart by at least a dozen of Gorion's minions. The great tree trunk was cast over in iron. I wondered how long our gates would hold against a battering ram like that. Not long, I shouldn't wonder.

We were doomed. Anyone could see that. If only there was something we could do to hold off the fall of our capital. If only there was someone who was strong enough to kill Gorion. But one look at that monster and I knew no Elf in all of Karaphyllon could ever kill him.

The Elf generals shook themselves out of their shock and into order. They began barking out orders to the warriors on the battlements. I had no idea what I was supposed to do. I was no soldier. I wasn't even carrying a sword. The captains would probably make me leave, go hide some place in the city. And after a look at the army we faced, that was all I wanted to do. Or better yet, run away from the city. Escape.

But it was too late. There was no escape for me now.

This was the end.

I took one last look at the approaching army, and ran.

CHAPTER 16

THE SIEGE BEGINS

Alec

I paced the floor of Lord Cedgewick's study, fingering the hilt of my newly mended sword at my belt. I had picked it up from Carlel's earlier this week. He'd said since Gwynneth had never had time to finish it, he had taken it upon himself to make sure it got finished. He was glad I had thought to pick it up before the siege began.

Gwynneth's father was beside himself with worry when I'd shown up on his doorstep a few days ago with the news that his daughter hadn't arrived at my house. I was at my wit's end with fear for her life.

I'd done my best to comb the city for her, even ridden Caspian around the nearby countryside, looking for any sign that she had gotten on a coach and that it had been waylaid on the road. I'd questioned the coach station until I was blue in the face, but they couldn't tell me much.

There had been so many ellassens fleeing the city, they had seen several that fit Gwynneth's description.

Now Gorion's army was here, right outside our gates, and we had bigger problems to face than my missing betrothed.

"You should go see how close they are to the main gate," Lord Cedgewick said from where he sat back in his desk chair. "It'd give you something to do then just pace and fret about Gwynneth."

I stopped in my tracks, meeting his eyes. "Are you not concerned about her, too, sir?"

From the stiff way he sat, I knew he feared for her. But the way he was pouring over the maps and plans for the battle here in his house, rather than with King Ethele in the war room, told me he had bigger things on his mind than his missing daughter.

I was worried about the battle too, but I couldn't seem to shake Gwynneth from my thoughts. If she was still alive somewhere, I had to find her, bring her back home, where she would be safe from Gorion's army. I didn't dare think aloud my worst fear, that she was lying dead somewhere, never to be found.

He looked up at me, tears pricking his eyes. "You know, I fear the worst has happened." His voice was husky, and he cleared his throat. "I must move on. Gorion is on our doorstep and there will be a battle either today or tomorrow. I have matters of state to concentrate on. You do too. I suggest you go out and check on the enemy."

I stood to attention. He knew I meant to fight in the battle. I'd said so all along. Now he meant for me to follow through with my intentions. "Yes, sir," I said.

It took a good forty minutes to make it to the main gate. They had barricaded many of the roads, and I kept having to find side routes to make my way through. I climbed the steps to the wall and joined the other warriors who stood along the wall watching the enemy. The archers had arrows nocked, waiting for the Throes to get within range.

They were almost here. Their army was running up to the wall. Their lighter infantry, carrying light ladders, was almost in arrow range.

"Steady!" the captain of the archers bellowed from where he stood near the end of the line.

I rushed past the archers and took my place in line next to the other swords-elves.

Right behind their light infantry rolled their battering ram, an iron tipped log made from a thick tree. It hung from chains attached to roof supports, which were attached to a mainframe with wheels for mobilization. The Throes were pushing it way too fast toward our gate. This was a siege engine that would work well. How long would our gates withstand such a thing?

"Fire!" the captain of the archers cried. "Take out the battering ram before it reaches the gate!"

A flurry of arrows zipped from the bows along the wall, many meeting their targets. But where one Throe fell, another quickly moved in to take its place. They swarmed so thickly around the battering ram that it wouldn't matter if we took out a hundred of them. They would still reach our gates with plenty of manpower left.

Then it was at the gate. I saw the Throes swing the battering ram backward, heard the massive thud of its iron cap hitting our heavy wooden gates. The ground shook at the impact.

I didn't have much time to pay attention to the next blow of their battering ram because the Throes with the ladders had reached the wall and were slinging their ladders against it. I scurried to join several Elves trying to push the nearest ladder down, away from the wall. Grunting and straining, I pushed with all my might alongside the others, but the Throes holding the bottom of the ladder were strong and the ladder held. First one hairy head emerged, followed by more and more, until the wall was swarming with Throes.

I drew my sword and fought off one Throe, then another. As soon as I killed a monster, another one would take its place. It was hard to keep my footing on the wide wall as more and more Throes came, pressing in, pushing me closer to the edge, trying to make me fall into the city.

Then two Throes were upon me at once. The warrior Elves surrounding us were busy fighting their own foes.

I ducked and dodged out of the way as best I could, but there was little space to move away on the crowded wall walk.

I parried a blow from one and ducked into a low squat to avoid the blade of the other. Then, still in a squat, I drove my sword into the lower abdomen of the first Throe. It fell back with a screeching howl that hurt my ears. I jumped to my feet and sliced off the second Throe's head with one strong, well-aimed sweep. Its body fell prostrate as its head went rolling along the walkway.

I picked up the severed head and hurled it at the nearest Throe. The monster snarled at me, catching the head and throwing it back. I ducked out of the way of the Throe head, which pitched over the side of the wall and dropped into the city. I heard someone wail from down below and hoped I hadn't just injured one of my own.

"Don't like heads being thrown around?" I taunted him.

He replied by lunging for me, fangs snapping. I jumped out of the way and circled him, waiting for him to let his guard down and give me an opening. I had to kill this Throe and quickly; more monsters were still pouring over the wall. The view from my periphery told me most of the Throes were meeting their deaths at the hands of the warriors on the wall. Good. At least we were winning so far.

The Throe lunged in for an attack, and I stepped out of the way, noticing how he left his left side wide open when he lunged. I'd just have to wait for him to do it again and hit him on that side to take him down.

I feigned a thrust, but didn't follow it through, pulling back as he stepped away, hoping to antagonize him enough to lunge at me again.

He lunged. I stepped right and plunged my sword into his left side before he had time to recover. He fell without a cry. His yellow eyes remained filled with hate as the life drained out of them.

I fought on the wall for what seemed like hours. Every time I thought we had killed enough Throes to gain the advantage, I looked up to realize that more monsters were still coming over the ledge. I was getting tired. I needed to rest, needed to find a way off this wall. But there was no break. No way off this wall. I had to keep fighting. Or die.

———◦✦◦———

I took a swig of water from the wooden cup a fanwas handed me, keeping my eyes on the wall up above. The fighting on the wall had been fierce, but somehow I'd made it down to take a break. Other warriors had quickly replaced me. Fresh ones, waiting on the stairs to go up and join the fight.

My legs felt like jelly, and I was grateful for the respite. Another boom from their battering ram sounded, and my eyes jumped to our Elves holding the beams to support the gate as the ellases were pushed back a few inches. They regrouped and braced themselves, waiting for the next jarring swing of that ram. At least they hadn't broken through our gates yet. That was one thing to be thankful for.

I looked back up at the wall where Throes still poured over the sides of the stone masonry. The Elves on the wall fought ferociously. One swordsman was cutting down Throe after Throe, holding his own. Another, an archer, stood near the city edge of the wall, firing at the Throes as they came up the ladder. Those Throes fell, either over our side of the wall, where our swords-elves finished them off, or they fell off the wall completely. Others weren't faring as well. I saw too many Elves down, injured or already dead. If only we could push their ladders back down, send them falling to their deaths.

My heart still galloped, and my breaths came in adrenaline-filled gasps. I took one more swig of water, trying to catch my breath, willing the soreness away in my legs and arms. They needed me up there. I had to recover enough to go join the fray again. I was a lord, yes, but an Elf warrior, just like the rest of them. By the Mighty One, I would go up there and do my duty for my country and for the world.

Thrusting the half-drunk cup of water at the fanwas, I pulled out my sword and stalked toward the stairs. I took a few more deep breaths, preparing myself for what I would face up there. Then I dashed up the stairs, taking them two at a time, and rejoined the fight.

⸺❖⸺

We were winning. The gates still held, but just barely. Their ram had been pounding at our doors for over two hours, making them weaker and weaker. We were winning as the skies grew dark and darker, holding our own on the wall, killing Throe after Throe after Throe. Pitching bodies over the edge of the wall back onto the battle plains as they piled up on the wall walk. There was so much blood and hair and muck. I was spattered in both black and red blood, but uninjured, thank the Mighty One. My shoulder was sore from swinging and thrusting my sword, but I continued from my position on the wall. We had to finish this thing, get to the end of the killing, and push our enemy to retreat.

Then it happened. There was a sickening, splintering crack of broken wood, and a groaning, shrieking of snapped metal. They had broken through the gates.

I looked down into the city where a few companies of soldiers stood, waiting for this moment—the moment when they would defend the city from the marauding Throes.

The Throes poured through the crack in our gates. The fissure grew wider and wider as more and more of the monsters scrambled through. Straight bright Elvish swords met the jagged black ones the Throes carried. Down below was chaos as the hoard of snapping, snarling Throes quickly swallowed up our companies of warriors.

There weren't enough. The ellases in those few companies weren't enough Elves to hold back the swarm.

I ran up to one of the commanders on the wall.

"We need more Elves down below!" I shouted, panting out the words. "Those ellases don't stand a chance with how few we have. Must send more elves down from the wall."

The commander knew who I was. Knew I was a lord. He glanced below, then gave me a quick nod.

"Take a company and go join the fight," he said, slapping me on the shoulder.

I nodded, then shouted orders to the ellases surrounding me. Soon, we were scrambling down the stairs and falling upon the enemy in the streets.

CHAPTER 17

FIGHTING WITH...A BLACKSMITH'S HAMMER?

Gwynneth

I ran pell-mell through the streets, heading back toward the blacksmith shop. It was so hard to turn away, but I needed to regroup and figure out what I was going to do. There must be something useful I could do, but what I'd just seen disoriented me. I couldn't think straight.

Within half an hour, I was back at the forge, rushing up the stairs to my little room and locking the door behind me. I sat on the bed, trembling, holding my head in my hands. I don't know how long I sat there, unable to do anything.

Soon, I heard the shouts and cries of battle far in the distance. I hoped the Throes hadn't already breached the walls with their siege engines. Thankfully, the forge was on the opposite side of the city as the main gate, the entrance

Gorion would focus most of his effort on. It would take some time for the enemy to make its way here. I was safe for a while. At least I hoped so.

The sounds of the battle made me sick to the stomach. Had I really wanted to go out there with a sword and join that melee? What was I thinking? Obviously, like an ellassen who had never seen war before. How foolish I was!

I went to the window and peered out, but of course I could see nothing but the city wall. My one window looked out toward the back of the city, not the front where the battle raged. I would have to go outside if I wanted to see anything. I just wished I had a weapon in here with me. There was no way I could go out there without a weapon. Perhaps there was a leftover sword in the shop below. Would it be risking too much to sneak down there and see?

I listened to the sound of the fighting for a few seconds—the fearful screams of the Elves and the guttural cries of the Throes they fought—and decided that they were still many blocks away, near to the city entrance, maybe still up on the wall.

Chaos. That's what it sounded like.

I would have to chance going downstairs and trying to find a weapon. I slowly unlocked the door, which opened with a loud click. The door swung open with a creak that made all the hair stand straight up on the back of my neck and I jumped at the sound. I knew I was too far from where the battle raged to be heard, but my nerves were on edge.

I peered around the door and looked outside. Dark clouds roiled in the sky, threatening rain, which would eliminate the ability of our archers on the walls. The din of battle was so much louder out here, I wanted to cover my ears to get away from it. A sickly stench permeated the air already, even this far away from the fight. I gagged, covering my nose with a handkerchief as I ran down the steps to the smithy.

Master Carlel had closed the shop doors and locked them, but thankfully he always kept a spare key buried in the dirt by the door. I felt around for it, and opened the shop door. Without the fire, and with all the windows closed and boarded up to prepare for the attack, it was completely dark in here. I opened the door wide, letting in a little bit of light, enough for me to see by, then began my search for a spare sword. Perhaps Master Carlel hadn't been able to get all the swords we'd made to the soldiers in time.

My search was in vain. Master Carlel had done his job well. There were no extra swords; the soldiers had needed all of them. So I grabbed the next best thing, my trusty iron hammer, and made my way back outside.

The sound of the battle was getting closer by the minute, letting me know we were losing. If they needed my help at all, now was the time. I swallowed back the bile that came to my throat at the thought of fighting against Gorion or his Throes, and took a deep breath, which just filled my nose with the awful smell of death. Coughing from the choking smell, I stood up and ran toward the sound of battle, hammer in hand.

I was only an ellassen, but they needed all the help they could get. All I could hear were the screams of dying Elves in my ears. The sound sickened me, but also strengthened my resolve to fight alongside the Elf warriors. I had found my courage, and I would do anything I could to stop those screams of death, even if I died in the process. My death would be worth it if it helped to defend my world from Gorion, this Shadow of death.

At the sound of battle, my heart beat quicker as I ran down the streets. My breath came in quick gasps as adrenaline pumped through my veins. Nervous, excited, and fearful, I just hoped I'd be able to keep my wits about me enough that I was a help to the Elves already fighting, and not a hindrance.

Even though it was broad daylight, dark, unnatural clouds covered the sun. A murky haze filled the air, making it hard to breathe. It smelled like magic, but not the kind I was used to working with. This smell was threatening, burning, suffocating.

How long will we last against such power? I wondered. I hoped it would rain. Anything to wash away this awful magic permeating the air.

The streets were all chaos when I reached the part of the city where the battle raged. Everywhere I looked I saw Elves lying on the ground, either injured and dying, or already dead. The streets ran red with blood, the blood of my people.

There were too many Throes inside the city walls. How had this many breached our walls already? The gates still held. Had they all come over the wall? I thought the walls of Trescone were stronger than that. The well-trained and formidable warriors placed along the walls should have been able to hold them off.

The monsters were even more horrible close up. Their bodies looked like huge, overgrown apes, while their heads were the heads of wolves. Bright, sharp fangs were set in their muzzles. They were snarling ferociously. I saw them using their black, razor-sharp swords as well as their teeth and claws for fighting.

My heart froze at seeing them so near, and my blood ran cold. How could I even hope to injure monsters like these? Someone had obviously bred them to kill all good things in the world.

I gripped my hammer tighter in my hands until my knuckles were white and my fingers ached with the effort of holding my makeshift weapon. I stood there, on the edge of the battle, staring at the Elf warriors who fought valiantly against the enemy. Thankfully, there was no sign of Gorion in this part of the city. He must be fighting somewhere else. Maybe not even inside the city yet.

A Throe saw me and charged, giving a howl so piercing it made my ears throb. I stared it down as it ran toward me, its mouth wide open, its yellow fangs dripping with either saliva or venom. I didn't want to find out which. My feet were glued to the cobblestones beneath me, frozen, too afraid to do anything. My eight-pound hammer hung uselessly in my small, ellassen arms.

Then the monster was upon me, and something in me snapped back to life. I raised my hammer, ready to defend myself.

I had the advantage of height, as the Throe was not very tall, but I could tell it was stronger than me. The creature raised its sword over its head in both hands and charged, ready to cleave off my head.

I waited until the monster was upon me, then blocked it. One single, elegant stroke that changed everything.

My hammer redirected the Throe's sword off its course. Its weapon veered to the left with such force that the monster went tumbling to the ground.

It rolled over twice, then sprang back up, sword in hand, ready for action.

But I was ready too.

I ducked out of the way a few times as it swung its weapon at me in practiced arcs. Then I saw my opportunity and lunged in before it could get its sword up, jabbing my hammer at its head. Iron met bone, and my enemy fell to the ground with a thud, breathing its last. One more blow to put it out of its misery. The monster was dead.

Another was upon me before I had a chance to catch my breath. I ducked out of the way, then swung my hammer at its skull, missing my mark. Then a second Throe joined the first in its fight against me.

I kept hard at it, mostly ducking and dodging now, trying to beat back two Throes at once. I stepped out of the way of a malicious cut. The monster's yellow eyes burned with bloodlust. I spun and parried the second Throe's blow with my hammer, wishing to the Mighty One that I had two weapons. It would make things so much easier.

With a curious flick of my wrist, I swung my hammer in a backhand stroke and disarmed one of the monsters. Lunging forward as fast as I could before the other Throe attacked again, I smashed my dark hammer into its face. It made a dull, sickening thud. The unarmed Throe fell down and didn't move.

The second Throe's sword arced through the air, coming straight for me. I ducked my head and rolled out of the way, springing up with my hammer, ready to strike once more.

The fight with the Throes continued for an hour. I heard Elves screaming in the distance, the clash of metal on metal, of metal on flesh, of wounded, dying things, Elves and Throes alike. And still, it went on.

I danced the great dance of war alongside the other Elf warriors. My hammer sang with sickening thuds to skulls. Throes cried out, their garbled, unearthly voices screaming in pain, pain that I was inflicting.

Here, it didn't matter that I was an ellassen. It mattered that I had a weapon, and that I knew how to use it. It was life and death out here. But mostly death.

I looked up from killing what must have been my fifteenth Throe. My hands were bloodied and muddied, my dress torn at the knees, the bottom half ripped clean off in the fray. An ellas was staring at me from across the crowded street, his eyes wide as he realized I was an ellassen. He gave the slightest shake of his head, as if he couldn't believe he was seeing an ellassen on the battlefield, fighting with a blacksmith's hammer, of all things.

I didn't have time to stare back. I shrugged my shoulders at the ellas, then smashed my heavy hammer into the head of the Throe running toward me before it could get its weapon up. It crumpled to the ground, its face smashed in, dead.

Then another Throe was upon me, and all thoughts of that ellas pausing from the fight to stare at me flew from my brain like a bird outflying a storm.

The creature cut with his sword. Rapid, heavy strokes, as I worked hard to duck out of the way of each one. I didn't have time in between to deal any offensive strokes myself, like I had with the other Throes. Honestly, I felt myself tiring. My eight-pound hammer was heavy in my hands, and it hadn't been a moment before.

I backed away from the Throe as it advanced toward me. Glancing behind me, I realized it was trying to corner me against a house. I jumped to the side, away from the building and out toward the street. I caught the creature off guard just long enough to deliver an off-kilter blow to its skull with my hammer.

It faltered for a second, then regained its balance and continued to attack me. My eyes went wide. The other Throes had fallen at my blows. This one didn't. I cursed myself for delivering such a weak, unbalanced blow. Knowing that I would do better with a sword than with my blacksmith's hammer, I leaped away again, and grabbed a sword from a fallen Elf nearby. Gritting my teeth, I willed my weariness away and determined to deliver hard, accurate blows to every Throe from now on. I had a sword now; I was even more deadly than before.

The creature slowly pushed me away from the melee and down an empty street. It rained blows down on my head the whole time. I kept backing up, getting out of the way, looking for a chance to parry one of his strikes.

I could tell that my blow had harmed it a little. After giving so many quick strokes, the creature's cuts were slower and not as accurate. I saw my chance to parry its strike and took it, redirecting its sword away from my body. But the monster was good at defense, too. Every blow I gave it, it defended with its sword or ducked out of the way.

My body was tiring now, too. My parries were delayed, and the creature's strikes left no room for me to go on the offensive with my new weapon. I couldn't hold my own much longer. The adrenaline coursing through my veins wasn't helping either. I could feel the energy seeping out of me faster than usual, and I couldn't seem to catch my breath, which slowed me down even more. I didn't know how much longer I could hold out against this opponent.

CHAPTER 18

FIGHTING FOR DEAR LIFE

Gwynneth

Time stood still as I fought for my life. The hazy sky grew thicker as more dark clouds rolled in. I could feel the storm that was about to pour down on us. I just hoped it would hold off an hour longer. We had to get as far as we could in defeating the enemy before the rain hampered us. And we couldn't afford to lose the aid of our archers on the walls.

I got in a few more good, offensive strikes on my enemy. Each one slowed it down more and more, but it never let me get near enough to injure it. Fortunately, I had blocked all its blows that I'd been too slow to move out of the way for, which surprised me. My foe was staggering after every blow it gave now, trying to take me down. Its breath came in wheezing gasps. I was sure one last blow to its head or chest, and it would be done for.

I waited for my chance, still backing up to avoid its strikes, still parrying its blows when I could as it grew weaker and weaker before my eyes. I just hoped my own strength would hold out longer than its. My sword felt so heavy in my hand. It was made for an ellas much stronger than me. Then my opportunity came, and I thrust my sword into its chest.

The monster fells to its knees, howling in pain. I withdrew my sword, and it lay gasping on the ground, still trying to gather enough strength to deliver another blow at me as it bled out. I hit it one more time, and it lay flat on the ground as its last breath left its body.

I stepped back, breathing heavily, every muscle in my body aching with the exertion it had taken to kill this one Throe. How was I going to be able to do this all day, perhaps for several days? I was already too tired to go on.

I looked down the side street, toward the main fray. It was all hand-to-hand combat here in these tighter streets, every Elf for himself, defending against one if not two or three enemy Throes at once. I wondered if the city would survive until sunset with how many Throes had already breached the walls.

Heavy footfalls sounded behind me, and I whirled around. Another monster was coming right at me, sword up above its head, holding it with both hands, ready to cleave my head in two.

I don't know where I found the strength to defend myself, but I somehow kept the monster at bay as it cut his ugly black sword at me repeatedly in overhand sweeping arcs. It snarled at me so ferociously, I stepped back more in fear of getting bitten than of being stabbed.

I ducked and leaped and parried, over and over again, anything to stay alive. The monster drove me further and further away from the main battle. The streets grew quieter, and all I could hear were my own gasping breaths, the monster's ferocious snarls, and the snapping of its fangs.

This part of town was deserted, with no one nearby to help me. What would I do when I lost all my strength? My parries were becoming slower and sloppier. I couldn't allow this monster to brutally murder me in my own city.

I gathered my strength and got a few quick offensive strokes in, flailing my weapon at it, but I was too far away to hit it.

"You." Strike. "Will." Strike. "Not." Strike. "Win!" I screamed at the Throe through gritted teeth. It backed up, avoiding my swinging sword as I advanced.

My shoulders were aching, and my wrists felt weak. I willed myself to keep up my attack, even though my arms were numb with tiredness.

We'd been fighting for so long. This Throe had pushed me far away from everyone else. The monster seemed still at full strength too, barely even winded. Meanwhile, desperate, ragged breaths fell from my mouth and sweat poured down my face and neck, falling into my eyes, making them smart and sting. I was half blinded by my own tears. I could barely see to block my enemy's blows.

Then the worst came. My sword had been getting heavier and heavier in my hands by the minute. My ability to step out of the way of its sword was getting sloppier and sloppier, and I knew my end was near. There was no way I could stand against this monster. It gave a powerful, sweeping stroke, and I didn't get my sword up in time. Its sword sliced across my chest.

There was an instant searing pain, hot like fire, and I cried out, stumbling backward. The monster grinned wickedly at me and snapped its fangs once more to scare me. It barely gave me a second to recover from the sword stroke before attacking me again. This time I was able to block it, but just barely. Its blow nearly knocked me off my feet.

If I had fallen, it would have killed me within seconds. But thankfully I kept my feet, staggering wildly, trying to find my balance. I wondered if I turned and ran, if I could outrun it until I escaped to safety. But where would I hide to get away from this monster? I didn't know.

I shook my head. Running would not work here. I had to stand my ground until either it, or I, was dead. Only then could I run from the battle. I gritted my teeth, and gripped my sword harder. I would see this through.

The Throe came at me with powerful sword strokes, trying to drive my injured body to the ground where it could stamp the life out of me easier. I refused to give in.

"Die, you beast!" I screamed as I continued to do my best at blocking its heavy blows. But I knew I would not last much longer. The end was near. If only someone would come to my rescue.

My strength was gone now. I held my sword feebly in my shaking hands, willing myself to keep going. I would not let this monster be the death of me.

Swinging my sword this way and that, I moved toward it as it stepped away, failing to meet the enemy's sword or contact a part of its body. The flat of its sword came crashing down on my head. I staggered under the blow and dropped to my knees, looking helplessly up at my enemy, who just snarled at me, no sign of mercy in its eyes.

I had worn no helmet or armor, and I could feel the gash its sword had made in my head. The blood ran down my back and face, and I was instantly light-headed. So, this was how I would meet death.

I stared up at the monster, its sword raised for the final killing blow, and something snapped in my brain. I would not let this monster kill me.

Just as its sword started arcing down toward me, its torso completely unprotected, I pierced my sword into its belly. It toppled over, blood gurgling from its mouth as its body convulsed, thrashing wildly.

My breath came in ragged gasps as my body gave out. Crumpling to my knees, dizzy and disoriented, I raised my eyes to see three more Throes coming straight at me.

"No," I whispered through my cracked lips. They were nearly upon me.

⸺⬥⸺

Alec

I rushed down the stairs, taking them two at a time, followed by the company of Elves the commander ordered to follow me. We were down at the bottom, and I plunged into the fray, sword raised.

Attacking the nearest Throe, metal rang on metal as it parried my blow. I staggered back, surprised at its quick reflexes. It narrowed its eyes at me and bared its fangs. Then it lunged for me.

I jumped back. It would take more to kill this monster down here on the ground than the fighting on the wall. Everything was so crowded up there, down here we had more space to fight, things were harder.

It lunged again, and I stepped out of the way. How had it gotten me on the defensive? I had attacked it first. Obviously, this was a monster who knew how to fight.

I parried a few more blows, then saw an opening for an attacking blow. I took it. My sword plunged into its sword arm shoulder. Blood spurted from the wound, and it fell to its knees, screaming in pain. One more blow and it was felled for good.

Excellent timing too, for two more Throes were upon me. I struck one in the gut with my sword, pulling it free as quick as I could to roll out of the way of the other Throe's strike. Springing back to my feet, I turned to face my enemy, my eyes narrowed, teeth bared. I would not let these monsters take me down.

I fought for what seemed like an hour, taking down Throe after Throe. More monsters kept pouring in through the breech in our gate, pushing us further and further back into the city streets. It was every man for himself, and nothing but mud, blood, and chaos in the hand-to-hand combat.

Then, just as I felled yet another Throe on a side street about three blocks down from the main gate, I heard an ellassen scream.

By the Mighty One, I hoped an ellassen wasn't caught out here in the battle. I pushed the Throe off the tip of my sword, and it toppled to the ground. Then I was rushing toward the sound of that scream. I couldn't leave a helpless ellassen to fend for herself against these beasts.

I dashed down one side street, then another. She screamed again, which sent the blood rushing to my face and left my heart pounding in my chest. I had to reach her in time.

There she was, in a side street, far from the rest of the battle, pinned against the side of a building with three Throes rushing toward her.

She carried a sword, and I stumbled back, wide-eyed. I knew her.

It was Gwynneth.

⊹

Gwynneth

At that moment, someone rushed to my aid with a mighty shout. His sword met the first Throe's as it arced toward my body, ringing through the air as metal struck metal. My head snapped up, and I was taken aback. It took me several minutes to realize what had happened. I was so dizzy I couldn't see very well, could barely make out that my rescuer was a tall, muscular ellas. Someone had found me at last and was here to help.

The Elf warrior finished the monsters in a matter of seconds. He gave a few well-aimed strikes at the beasts, moving like someone I knew, but through my hazy vision I couldn't place this ellas. The Throes howled their death cries and fell, defeated. When I saw my enemy fall, that was it. I fell face first to the ground and felt the blackness wash over me.

CHAPTER 19

Healing

Gwynneth

I awoke several hours later in my bedroom at home. Bandages wrapped my chest and head, and I felt woozy from the aching throb of the wounds, dulled by whatever salve they applied while bandaging me up. Someone had even washed the sweat and blood of battle from my tired body. My head felt stuffed with wool, and I whimpered from the pain.

Alec was by my side in an instant. He took my hand and pressed it between his own. Worry clouded his entire face, and I also thought I saw disappointment in his eyes.

"Alec?" I asked, my voice hoarse from all the shouting I'd done during the battle. "What are you doing here? Why aren't you back in Annwythel?" I forgot for a moment what Master Carlel had told me about how Alec was staying at my father's house again.

"I came back here when you didn't arrive at my home," he said. "I had to find you. Make sure you were safe." He looked down at our entwined hands, rubbing my knuckles in little comforting circles. "You don't know how worried I've been about you, Gwynneth," he said, looking back up at me. "You don't know how I felt when I saw that Throe upon you about to kill you."

"Thank you for rescuing me," I murmured, marveling that it was he who had found me when I was at the end of my strength.

That it was Alec set my heart beating faster. He had rescued me, just like a prince rescues a princess in all the fable stories I'd read as a fanwassen. It was too romantic for words. I willed myself to think straight about this. I would not fall in love with Alec just because he had rescued me from certain death, betrothed though we may be.

"I can't believe you were the ellas who rescued me." My mouth went dry at the thought. I couldn't take my eyes off him.

"Well, I couldn't let that monster kill you, now, could I?" he said, meeting my gaze with a sad, worried smile.

I laughed a little, which made my chest ache, and I coughed. Then I couldn't stop coughing. I sat up in the bed, which hurt more than I'd like to admit, and Alec gently patted my back and helped me take a sip of water. When the last coughs subsided, I sank back against the pillows, wincing at the pain the coughing had caused.

"Well, I'm glad you were there. I don't know what I would have done if no one had come," I whispered, a lump coming into my throat as I thought back to how I had stared death in the face.

"Whatever possessed you to hide away in the city and join in the battle?" he asked me, his blue eyes stern now, almost angry. "That was a foolhardy thing to do, Gwynneth. I'm disappointed in you." His voice softened at his last sentence, as if he didn't want to voice it, but had to.

My face reddened at his rebuke.

"Well, I'm not disappointed in myself," I said, meeting his eyes and lifting my chin. I'd made the decision that I thought was best at the moment. How dare he rebuke me. "I thought I would be more useful here defending my home than running away to avoid the war." I looked away, unable to meet those stern eyes. They reminded me too much of my father those days before the betrothal ceremony.

"It wouldn't have been running away," he said.

"Yes, it would have," I bitterly replied. I still couldn't look at him.

"Don't argue with me, dearest," he said, his voice gentle. "Your father and I were just trying to keep you safe. We just wanted what was best for you." He looked down and released my hands, sighing.

"And what will happen now?" I asked, bringing my gaze back to look at his bowed, defeated head.

"I don't know. Your father and I still have to decide. While the city is under attack, I don't think we'll be able to escape." He pressed his lips together, looking back up at me. His eyes were so clouded with worry. "For now, we'll just hide out here and hope we're not discovered."

"I see," I said. I was a little disappointed that I had been injured on the first day of fighting. But I had killed a Throe. Many Throes. I knew my efforts had helped my people win this war, and I felt pride rising in my chest at my courage.

"It's late. Get some rest," he said, rising. He wasn't proud of me at all, not the way his shoulders hunched dejectedly. I had disobeyed his wishes and disappointed him in the process. The pride for my heroic actions dissipated, leaving me feeling empty.

My head hurt and I tried not to cry as he stood, staring at me lying in my bed, helpless. I was too hurt to move. At least I had gotten to fight a little. But even if I recovered, Alec and Father would get me out of the city as soon as they could.

He bent over the bed and brushed my brow with his lips, then left the room, taking the candle with him, leaving me lying there in the dark. My heart pounded away like a drum at the thought that he had just kissed me. It was so forbidden by our culture, and yet he'd done it.

The pain of my wounds disappeared for a few seconds as the elated feeling of being kissed for the first time filled my mind, making me giddy. Then the pain returned.

I don't know how long I lay there, unable to move because of my wounds, in too much pain to sleep. Then, as the sky began lightening for the morning, I fell asleep.

—◈✦◈—

I woke up to the sun shining in my eyes through the gap in my bedroom curtains. By the way it shone through my window, it was nearly midday. I tried to move my head to get out of the sun's glare. A jolting pain shot through my entire body, and I screamed in pain.

Someone pounded up the stairs two at a time and rushed into my bedroom, causing the door to bang against the wall, which just made my head hurt worse.

I moaned and grabbed my aching, bandaged head.

Alec was by my side in an instant, grasping my hand and looking down at me worriedly.

"Are you all right, Gwynneth? What happened?" he asked, the concern dripping from his voice.

"I'm fine," I answered bravely, but I felt far from it. My voice sounded so weak. "I just tried to move, that's all. Can you close the curtains, please?" I asked, squinting up at him. "By the Mighty One, that sun is bright."

He was over by the window, rushing to do my bidding before I finished speaking, closing the curtains with such vehemence I was sure he would tear them off their rod. He came back to my side, pulling up a chair and taking a seat once his task was finished.

"Better?" he asked, taking my hand. His touch, forbidden by the laws, was so gentle. I didn't want him to stop.

"Yes. Thank you," I answered.

He sat there and silently stroked my hand, his eyes never leaving my face, while I stared back at him, trying to think of something else to say, but my head hurt too much for conversation. There was an awkward pause for several minutes. At least, I found it awkward. Alec seemed unphased by the silence.

"How's the battle going?" I asked.

"Well, they haven't reached us yet here by the palace, so our warriors must be holding them at bay nearer the main gates," Alec said.

"You're sure?"

"No. To be honest, I haven't gone searching for any news about how the battle is going. I've been too busy taking care of you." He withdrew his warm hand from my grasp, sighing and shaking his head in worry. "That was a stupid thing to do, Gwynneth. Joining the battle like some fool. Were you trying to get yourself killed?"

"You should be happy that I was the one doing most of the killing, instead of the other way round. Not all Elves fared as well as I did, you know." I tried to defend myself, thinking of the Elves I'd seen yesterday who had lost their lives, just lying there in the streets, blood pooling on the surrounding ground.

"Fared as well as you?" Alec repeated incredulously. There was no sign of the worried ellas from last night about him. He was angry. Angry at me for being so foolhardy and almost getting myself killed. "Look at yourself, lying in bed with extreme injuries." He waved a hand that encompassed all of me, and I felt so helpless lying in this bed, unable to move from the pain.

"Well, at least I'm not dead!" I shouted, making my head throb even more.

"You're not dead because I rescued you," he said, exasperated. "You should thank the Mighty One I was there when I was. If I hadn't been there, you would be dead by now. Remember that, Gwynneth."

I opened my mouth to reply, then closed it shut again. It would be foolish to say anything now. Not after a reprimand like that. I was ashamed of myself. I had gone into battle, hoping to be everyone's hero, and I had barely made it out alive myself. What an idiot I'd been.

"Now, can we speak of this no more?" he asked, his voice weary from our arguing. "I just want you to get well again. And the only way that will happen is if you rest and recover. Fighting with me won't help that at all, I'm sure."

I nodded, too embarrassed and upset to give a verbal reply, even though the nod made my head feel like someone had just cleaved it with an ax.

He left the room, giving one last disappointed look at me. I wondered if I'd ever win his respect back.

Alec thought I had been foolish to join in the fight. I thought I had been doing my duty. Acting the way a brave, courageous young ellassen should. But of course, there had been no other ellassens fighting. Fighting for our freedom was something left to the ellases. We ellassens were meant to stay home and take care of the fanwases and fanwassens. Keep the home fires burning bright.

I hadn't been foolish. I'd acted heroically joining the fight. Yes, a Throe had injured me. But they had injured many ellases, too. Many more had met death. I had not. I was still alive to live another day.

The next half hour or more, I spent trying to rest, but the whole time my head was spinning, trying to justify my actions and coming up with responses to imaginary conversations with Alec. All the conversations turned into arguments, somehow. I gave eloquent speeches explaining how my actions in joining the battle were right. But he never agreed. Not in one single, imaginary conversation. And I wondered if he would ever agree with my words in real life, or just shut me down with his own arguments, like he had this morning.

I felt stuck. Alec and I had never argued before. But I'd never run away from home and disobeyed my father before, either. And now that Alec and I were betrothed, I had also disobeyed him, which was a grievous way to start a relationship.

But there wasn't much I could do to mend what had been done. I was too headstrong. I hoped I could learn how to be a properly behaved ellassen. Otherwise, I'd be a failure at being Alec's wife. And I couldn't do that to him. He was a lord, and he deserved an ellassen who was good at fulfilling the role of a lord's wife. I just hoped I could live up to it one day.

My heart pitter-pattered in my chest as I realized what I had just thought. I wasn't thinking along the lines of getting out of this betrothal anymore. I was thinking of seeing it through. The thought excited me, but most of all, it terrified me. What would I be without my blacksmithing?

⋯⊰✦⊱⋯

Alec

I trudged down the stairs, kicking myself internally. I shouldn't have berated her a second time. That conversation would have gone so differently if only I'd kept my stupid mouth shut.

But I was so worried about her. She had screamed loud enough I'd heard her in the parlor with the door closed. I'd carried her in last night from the battle and seen Collette tend to her wounds until the old cook had shooed me out of the kitchen.

It's not proper for you to be looking at your betrothed in her state of undress. The old ellassen had scolded me.

At least she looked better now that she was cleaned up and well bandaged. But she was still so pale. How much blood had she lost, and how much time would it take to get her strength back?

The Throes could push our warriors deeper into the city at any time. I'd been there when they broke through the gates. It was only a matter of time before they were here, on our doorstep. And Gwynneth couldn't defend herself, not in her state. A steely resolve entered my heart. I would defend her. With my life.

What had I been thinking, berating her again, though? It was because she had scared me so. When I saw her in the battle, I froze a few seconds, too afraid for her to make any moves toward her. Then I'd whipped into action, running to her aid, anything to save her life.

I guess my fear was still coming through in my words and actions toward her. Now she was mad at me, and being surprisingly stubborn in defending herself. She was beautiful when she was mad, the way her cute face had gotten all flushed and she'd flashed her eyes at me. But no matter how beautiful she became in her anger, I needed to stay levelheaded and not provoke her. The last thing I wanted was for her to push herself away and not complete the betrothal.

I needed her now more than anything. Especially with us being stuck in this Throe-infested city. Whether we lived or died here, I needed her by my side. She was too precious to let go of. And too beautiful.

I felt like I knew now what I needed to offer Gwynneth. I would offer her the world.

CHAPTER 20

BRAVE OR FOOLHARDY?

Gwynneth

I stayed in my bedroom as long as I could stand. Alec was right. My body needed rest. I wanted him to come visit me again so I might say some of the things I had been thinking of saying to him all day. But I knew it wasn't proper for him to be in my bedroom, even if we were betrothed now. That was probably why he was staying away. Father had probably talked to him about it again.

After a good hour of lying there fretting, I couldn't stand it anymore. I sprang out of bed and got ready to go downstairs.

In reality, I moved quite slowly. Sitting up in bed with a groan, willing the pounding in my head to go away. Of course, it persisted like an annoying little fanwas who didn't know his manners, pounding away at my temples. Gingerly, I placed my feet on the wooden floor and felt a searing pain in my chest where that monster's sword had sliced me. I bit my lip to keep from crying out as I stood up. Practicing not showing signs of pain to my father and Alec began now.

I tucked my hair behind my ears and went over to the wardrobe, where I picked out a simple linen dress. It took me forever to take off my nightgown and put the dress on. I had to move slowly to keep from being in excruciating pain from my wounds and ended up taking several breaks because the pain was too much.

I was beginning to wonder if I'd make it downstairs before the midday meal was over. But I pressed on, intent on what I wanted to do.

Finally, I opened my bedroom door, fully dressed, my long brown hair done up in a simple brown hair net, no sign of the wild, unkempt braid from the battle, and began my descent down the staircase.

Why did the stairs have to be so steep? That was the one fault in this house. Steep stairs. I held back a groan as I painstakingly made my way down the steps. I was so dizzy; I hoped I wouldn't fall over.

After what seemed like twenty minutes, but was probably two, I was at the bottom of the steps and I hadn't fallen over. Proud of myself for managing this far, I made my way into the dining room where Father and Alec still sat at lunch. They were finished eating, and were just sitting with their empty plates before them, talking.

They both turned to me when I entered the room and slowly took my usual seat, looks of shock and surprise, then concern, on both their faces. I thought my father would seem angry with me, but the look in his face when our eyes met was one of sadness. I had disappointed him beyond words by running away from home, hiding in the city, then fighting in the battle.

"What are you doing down here?" Alec asked worriedly, half rising from his seat. "You should be up in your room resting."

"Honestly, Alec, I really don't think I'm the sort of ellassen who could spend all day in my room resting," I replied dryly, though my head throbbed so much I wished I could do just that. But I had to prove to them I was better than I felt. "This morning was bad enough. You can't make me stay up there."

"You're right," Alec answered with a sigh, sinking back down into his chair. "I can't seem to make you do anything. You know how strong willed you are, Gwynneth?" He was trying to sound lighthearted broaching the subject, but it still came out as an accusation that I could tell frustrated him.

"I'm aware of it," I said, glancing at Father, wondering if he would enter in this conversation.

I felt pretty proud of myself coming down here like this and holding my own. This conversation was going exactly how I imagined it would, and I was pleased I was getting to say some of the things I had imagined myself saying earlier this morning. It felt good to get it off my chest.

"I'm afraid this is an area you're going to have to work on, dearest," Alec said, lowering his voice and speaking more gently, his blue eyes earnest with me, ignoring the fact that Father was here at the table too and heard every word we spoke.

I pursed my lips, thinking up a response. His use of that term of endearment irked me, but I knew he was right. If we were going to marry and live peacefully with each other, I was going to have to become more compliant with his wishes. That is, if I couldn't form any plans of my own and figure a way out of this betrothal. I didn't even know if I wanted to find a way out of this betrothal anymore.

"Well, if that's something you wish for me to work on," I said with a shrug of my shoulders. That was a mistake. Pain from my chest wound shot up my neck and went straight to my head. I winced.

"Are you alright?" Alec asked.

He'd been observing me, and I had slipped, showing my pain to him. My heart sunk as I thought he would insist on sending me back upstairs to my room and, based on our conversation, I would have to agree, to practice being less strong willed.

"I'm fine." I managed a smile, and reached for the break-fast pastries on a platter in the center of the table.

He continued to stare at me, concerned as I ate my breakfast. I moved through the motions of eating extremely slowly, to avoid bringing on any more shooting pains from moving too fast. Being injured was horrible. And yet, somehow, it didn't discourage me from wanting to face battle again.

I was still very proud of myself for how well I did in the battle.

"Alec, did you see much fighting yesterday?" I asked when I was nearly finished with my pastry. It had occurred to me that since he'd rescued me from certain death there at the end, he must have been fighting too.

"Yes, I was in the battle the whole time," he said, biting his lip and looking down.

"You were in the battle the whole time. Fighting the whole time. And yet you told me it was foolhardy for me to fight?" I asked incredulously, bristling at this piece of news.

"Well, I'm not an ellassen," he stated, biting his lip and looking down at his empty coffee mug.

"Not an ellassen!" I shouted at him, anger rising in my chest, my eyes widening and nostrils flaring. "What are we ellassens? Useless? Good for nothing but bearing and raising the next generation of Elves?" I stared from him to Father, incredulous at his chauvinistic response, and beyond angry.

Father sat there in silence, awkwardly fingering the grain of the sturdy oak table, unwilling to enter the conversation and voice an opinion.

"I don't mean it like that, Gwynneth," Alec said, meeting my furious glare.

But I had already knocked over my chair in my haste to leave and was halfway out of the room, too blinded by rage to hear any sort of explanation.

He stood up and snatched my hand. I struggled to free myself from his grasp, clenching my jaw and refusing to look at him. My wounded chest felt on fire with the movement, but I didn't care.

"Gwynneth, please," he pleaded, still clutching my hand.

I had lost this fight. It hurt too much to pull my hand free, so I gave up.

"Don't take everything so offensively," he said.

"And why not?" I asked, trying not to shout, glancing back at Father, who remained silent in his chair at the head of the table. Part of me wished he would butt in, but Alec was my betrothed now. He had a say in my life just as much as Father did. "Why should I not be offended when you two do everything you can to stop me from doing the things that I love most? That I care for most? That I believe in most?" The hot tears sprang to my eyes as I spoke, threatening to spill over. I cleared my throat, willing the tears away. I would not let him see me cry.

"I..." Alec started, but obviously didn't know what to say. He hadn't been the one to end my apprenticeship with Master Carlel, nor had he been the one to force a betrothal date upon me.

I looked back at my father, whose fault it really was.

"Everything I do is to protect you, daughter," Father said, at last entering the conversation. He stood up and came around the table to stand by me. His eyes were stern as always, his words final. "I didn't want you close to the fighting because I didn't want this to happen to you." He indicated the bandages on my head and chest. "I didn't want to lose you too." He said the last bit in a whisper, and I glimpsed the pain he kept buried deep inside. Pain from losing Mother and Timithen all those years ago.

But I was too mad. "And you didn't want me to have an ellas's job," I retorted, ignoring that he was bringing Mother and Timithen into this argument. The fact that he sent me away a week before I finished my apprenticeship still burned red hot in my mind. He had tried to ruin everything I cared about. Everything I had worked toward the past three years. And that's all that mattered. "You don't want to protect me. You just want your will for my life over my own!" I screamed at him.

I placed both my hands on my father's chest and shoved him angrily. Pain erupted in my chest as I felt newly stitched skin pull. I cried out and fell to my knees in pain. Father bent down to help me, but I swatted his hand away.

"Don't touch me!" I said through gritted teeth.

Alec was at my side in an instant, his gentle hands on my waist, trying to keep me from falling prostrate. Even though I was mad at him, too for his unfeeling comment about gender roles, I allowed him to slowly help me up, the sharp pain in my chest throbbing.

"I think you should go back up to your room and rest," Alec said gently.

"No," I answered, shaking my head, which just made me dizzy. "Take me to the parlor. I can rest there."

Alec sighed. "Alright," he said, and did as I bid him.

I gave one last glare to Father as Alec and I left the room.

In a minute we were in the parlor, and he was easing me onto a couch. I wanted to lie down and rest my aching head, but I willed myself to just sit there. I felt pitiful, and I was in so much pain. That had been stupid of me to move that quickly out of the room, then shove my father. I had never acted aggressively toward my father. What had come over me?

I had no doubt my wounds were muddling my head, making me more emotional, unpredictable. Father and Alec were right. I needed to rest and recover, not give way to a silly argument, like what had just happened.

I was ashamed of myself for acting the way I had. Especially for pushing my father. It was humiliating, knowing that I would have to apologize to him later. Why was I always wrong, and Father, and now Alec too, were always right?

Alec took a seat in the chair across from the couch where I sat, and stared at me worriedly.

I felt the hot tears well up in my eyes, and though I willed them away, they came anyway and ran down my cheeks. I felt so miserable, both physically and emotionally.

Alec shifted in his seat and stared at the ground, the sight of me in tears obviously making him uncomfortable. He looked at a loss as to what to do. I was content when he did nothing but sit there and study the carpet. He glanced at me occasionally, a nervous look in his eyes, then he looked back down.

"Is there anything I can do to help?" he finally broke the silence. There was genuine concern in the tight expression on his face.

I pursed my lips and shrugged.

"I don't know. I feel terrible," I murmured, drying my eyes on my dress sleeve.

"I'm sure you'll feel much better in a few days," he replied, trying to smile at me. "Healing takes time."

"I just wanted to be brave," I said, bringing up why I had fought in the battle. "Wanted to do my part in the fighting."

"I know," he said lightly. "And you were brave."

"Then why did you call me foolhardy?" I asked, looking up at him helplessly.

He took a deep breath, looking down at the floor before he looked up and met my eyes.

"You don't know how scared I was when I saw you fighting that Throe in the street. You were all alone. There was no one nearby to help you. I knew you didn't have any strength left to fight. I could see how worn out you were. I knew it was about to cut you down. That scared me to death, the thought of losing you." He wiped his hands on his thighs, shaking his head. "I was just trying to protect you by sending you out of the city before the battle. You know that. I'm just sorry you thought it was for a different reason, and that it nearly got you killed," he finished, then looked back down at the carpet.

"I scared you?" I asked. It hadn't occurred to me that my actions would have scared him, that he already cared for me enough that the thought of losing me frightened him. It brought a good, warm feeling to my miserable heart.

He looked back up at me. There was no hesitation. "Yes."

"I'm sorry," I said. "That wasn't my intention. You know all I wanted to do was finish my apprenticeship. That's why I stayed. That's where I've been, at Master Carlel's, helping him finish the swords for the army. You must know how much it means to me?" I asked, unsure if he did or not.

"I think I'm beginning to see that," he said with a smile. "And you know what I think?"

I shook my head.

"I think I'm going to give you your own forge in Annwythel."

"I'd like that," I said, smiling back at him, hope rising in my chest at his words.

I'd never imagined he would say something like that. I'd thought I would have to end our relationship at the end of our year-long betrothal if I wanted to continue my blacksmithing trade. And he was willing to give me a forge. That spoke volumes to me, and my heart melted a little. But I held myself back. I couldn't just give my heart to this ellas that I didn't know very well. I needed to know him better before making my final decision.

"The week that you needed to finish your apprenticeship has passed," he pointed out. "Has Carlel given you your certificate of completion?"

"He's in the process of writing it up. I'm not leaving the city without that," I said testily.

He paused a minute, thinking before he replied. "Alright," he said. "But the minute you have your certificate, I want you on the next coach out of the city."

"Is it not too late to leave the city?" I wondered. No one had told me how the fighting was going. I just knew since we were so close to the palace that our district was one of the last districts in the city that the battle would reach.

"I hope it's not," Alec said, his voice grim.

We stared at each other, not willing to say what we were thinking. That if it was too late to leave the city, we might have just sealed our fate, and death awaited us soon. Gorion's army was formidable, greatly outnumbering our own. And those Throes were powerful beasts, cunning with a blade. If it was too late to escape from the city, we might very well end up on the tip of one of their black blades. Dead.

CHAPTER 21

NEWS OF THE SIEGE

Alec

I'd done it. I'd given her something she couldn't refuse. The thing that she desired above all else. Her own forge.

The soft, trusting look that came into her eyes when I told her was one I'd treasure forever. She'd looked excited, like she'd burst with joy. No signs of her anger toward me and her father, no signs of the moping ellassen I'd encountered since Lord Cedgewick made all those changes for her. Just pure, unbridled joy. That was the Gwynneth I knew from her father's letters. That was the ellassen I wanted to spend the rest of my life with.

Now all I needed to do was tell her my family's secret. I just hoped she wouldn't ridicule me for it. It was something we were all ashamed of. I just hoped once she heard, she wouldn't break off the betrothal.

It shouldn't break her trust in me, but the fear niggled in the back of my mind, anyway.

Gwynneth

I spent the rest of the day in the parlor, refusing to go upstairs to rest, even though Alec kept encouraging me to do so. I was too stubborn. I didn't want to show any signs of tiredness or pain, though I felt both.

So, we sat and talked. Despite him having stayed with us those few days before our betrothal, we hadn't talked much. Not the getting to know one another sort of talking. Every conversation had revolved around our work and the imminent threat of Gorion and his army. Now we really talked.

Alec told me a little about growing up as the only son to a Lord of the Council. The picture he painted of his father was of an ellas steeped in tradition and yet open to ideas outside of tradition. He always tried to see both sides to the many arguments that came up in the council meetings, and I knew I would have liked him.

I thought Alec must be a lot like his father as he fondly told me about the ellas, a gleam in his blue eyes. Alec had a good sense of duty about him, doing his work as a Lord of the Council faithfully. And he enjoyed it. I also knew that he had strong protective instincts from the way he had tried to get me out of the city before Gorion's army came.

And yet he had been quite the mischievous little fanwas. Often playing pranks on everyone, including his father and mother. How his younger sister had been his co-conspirator growing up, once she was old enough to do the stupid things he told her to do.

"And she never asked you why you wanted her to do that?" I asked, commenting on the story of when he and his sister had blown up a chicken coop.

"No," he said with a grin. "Mirith just did what she was told, no questions asked. She trusted me in everything, even when doing so got us both in trouble." He shook his head, smiling at the memories.

"Wait, did you say your sister's name is Mirith?" I asked, my throat going dry.

He nodded and smiled. "Why do you ask?" His smile faded. "Gwynneth, are you alright? You've gone pale," he said, his worried eyes on me.

"Mirith was my mother's name." I looked down, bunching and unbunching a bit of fabric of my pale green dress. "Father never told you?" I asked, looking up.

He shook his head, his face pinched. "Are you alright?"

I bit my lip and slowly nodded my head. "You just caught me off guard, that's all." I gave him a watery smile.

That meeting someone who shared my mother's name would bring up all this old grief hadn't even crossed my mind. I didn't even miss Mother as much as I missed Timithen. And yet my betrothed's sister shared her name.

"I suppose that piece of information is something I'll have to get used to," I said.

"I suppose so," he said, then launched into another outrageous story about him dressing up as a peasant and begging at his own kitchen door to get a snack one day. "I was completely covered in mud, and Cook didn't recognize me until I'd been eating a whole five minutes," he said, laughing.

I laughed along and realized he'd driven all my grief away. I smiled at him, grateful, and he grinned back and continued.

"There is this secluded lake with a huge waterfall we used to go swimming in during the summer. I'll have to take you there when we get to Annwythel." He broke off, looking at me as if he half expected me to get mad at his bringing up our inevitable trip to his home.

"If we can still escape the city," I added quietly.

Now that I was injured, I was thinking it might be better if I left the city. I just hoped I wouldn't have to leave it in a carriage all alone except for the driver. I hoped Alec would come with me.

"Yes. If that," he murmured. Then we fell into gloomy silence.

Our future looked bleak with the battle raging just a few streets away. When the house got perfectly still, I could hear the raging roar of battle. Oh, how I hoped we were holding our own.

"So, if we do marry at the end of this year-long betrothal," I began, and his head snapped up, blue eyes piercing mine, focused on my hopeful sounding words. "Where will we live? Will I move to Annwythel with you and live with you and your family?"

"Well, I've been thinking about it and—"

My father entering the room silenced him. Father was buttoning his jacket that he wore only when he left the house. No fancy council robes today. Just plain clothes, meant for traveling, not showing one's status in society.

"I'm going out. To get news," he stated, pausing as if he expected us to react.

There was a moment's silence as both Alec and I tried to think of an appropriate response. Here was my father, risking his life, to get news of how the battle was going. But then again, perhaps he would just go to the palace where, no doubt, King Ethele was being informed of the enemy's every move in his city. Father was like that, always taking the safer option.

"I hope you find out good news. And not bad," Alec said, looking up to meet my father's steady eye.

"The Mighty One be with you," I spoke the customary words of parting.

"And also with you," he returned with the customary response, meeting my eyes. Then, dipping his head briefly to both of us, he turned and left the house.

Even though Alec was with me, I suddenly felt more alone. Seen and unprotected. I shook the feeling away. Did I feel my father's protection of me as an ellassen that strongly? I frowned at the thought, disliking it.

"Something wrong?" Alec asked. He'd been watching me since my father had walked from the room.

"No," I said, looking up to meet his eyes while telling myself to quit frowning. "What were you saying before my father came in?"

"Um, I was going to say that I don't want to live with my mother and sister. Not when we're first..." he broke off, as if he couldn't bring himself to say the word. As if saying it would make it happen. And with him knowing I didn't feel for him in that way yet, he couldn't be that hopeful. Not yet. Not hopeful enough to speak of us actually marrying, as if it really would become our reality.

He pursed his lips and looked down. I could see the slight red creep along the tips of his pointed ears.

"So, you want to live alone, just the two of us?"

"As is customary," he murmured, glancing up at me briefly, then looking back down.

"But where? At Annwythel?" I asked, curious.

"Well, yes," he stated simply, as if that was an obvious answer.

But I didn't think it was obvious.

"But as a Lord of the Council, won't you have to make a lot of trips here to Trescone?" I pressed.

He nodded.

"Then wouldn't it make more sense to live here? Then we won't have to travel back and forth as much."

I was pressing the issue because deep down inside, I didn't want to leave my home, the city I knew so well. In fact, leaving it scared me. Especially with a near stranger like Alec.

He looked up at me then, a startled look in his eyes.

"I hadn't thought of that," he said. Then he quickly shook his head. "We couldn't do that. I'm Lord of Annwythel and expected to live there among the Annwythel Tribe. I can't just leave."

I wondered if part of his answer stemmed from the shared fear of not wanting to leave the home he'd grown up in too. But one of us would have to leave. And I knew in my heart it would be me.

⟡

I shifted uncomfortably in my seat in the parlor. We had been sitting there all afternoon, waiting for Father's return. Now it was well past supper time and I was getting nervous about the whereabouts of my father. A small trip to the palace shouldn't take more than an hour or two, and he had been gone twice as long as that. Despite how frustrated I was at him, he was still my father and I still loved him.

Alec sighed and looked at me, concerned.

"I wish you would go up to your room where you could rest. That's what your body needs, and you're not giving it that." He shook his head at me sadly, worry clouding his features.

"I've been getting plenty of rest sitting here all day," I obstinately replied, willing myself not to let the pain I was experiencing show.

"You should be lying down," he gently insisted. "You're dizzy and you have a headache, right?"

"How did you know?" I asked, astonished at his accurate guess. I'd been wishing I could go up to bed for the past hour, but I told myself when I was getting dressed that I would spend all day downstairs. I was just too stubborn.

"You might think you're good at hiding your symptoms, but they show," he answered, pressing his lips together. "Part of me wants to just carry you upstairs and force you to stay in your room. But then you would hate me forever and probably injure yourself further trying to fight me."

I smiled, knowing this would be my exact response.

"How do you know me so well already?" I asked, still smiling.

"Please just go upstairs and rest," he said, ignoring my question.

My smile slowly died, and I sighed and looked down. I knew I ought to oblige him, if only to make him feel better. Then I remembered that one of the first keys to being a good wife was obedience, and the rebellious part of me angered at the thought. I took a deep breath, willing my anger away. I needed to grow up. Now that I was betrothed to this ellas, I knew that meant taking the first step toward being his future wife and obeying his wish. Especially now that I was rethinking breaking off the betrothal in the end.

"Alright. You win," I said, slowly standing up. A wave of dizziness and nausea passed over me. Alec was instantly across the room, at my side, gently taking hold of my arm.

"Easy," he said, then led me out of the room and up the stairs.

He didn't let go of me until I crossed the threshold of my room. Then he dropped my arm and stayed in the doorway, doing the customary thing and not entering my bedroom.

I slowly sank down onto my bed and sat staring up at him, wondering why he had changed to formalities now, when he hadn't in the past.

"Your father talked to me about it," he said, reading the questioning look on my face. Then he stiffly said, "I can't come into your bedroom anymore. I'm sorry for trespassing before. I hope you can forgive me."

I felt a grin slowly spread across my face, then I laughed outright.

When he just continued to look at me, standing there in my doorway, every part of him stiff as a board, I quit laughing, feeling a little ashamed of my childish behavior.

"I'm sorry," I said. "I shouldn't have laughed. Of course I can forgive you."

"Well, I'll leave you to rest then," he said, wistfully lingering in the doorway.

"Oh formalities. What would we do without them?" I asked, my smile coming back.

I was glad when he smiled back at me, the light returning to his eyes.

"I'll see you at supper, when your father comes back," he said, and closed the door.

I lay back on my bed, arms tucked behind my head, thinking.

If nothing, he was an honorable ellas. One who respected my father's wishes. I had to give him credit for that.

⎯⋙✦⋘⎯

I stared at the clock all evening, willing the time to go faster, hoping Father would return soon. Part of me was worried about him. The other part of me thought it was boring and lonely being stuck up here in my room, my head pounding too much to even attempt reading a book or doing something else to pass the time. So I lay there, contemplating the sudden turn my life had taken when

Alec entered it two weeks ago. So many changes since then, and hardly any of them favorable.

Finally, after what seemed like an eternity, the clock told me it was time to hobble back downstairs to join Alec, and hopefully my father, for supper.

All the rest I'd gotten this evening must have done me some good, because I was noticeably faster going down the stairs and walking into the dining room.

I breathed a sigh of relief when I saw my father sitting in his usual place. I hadn't allowed myself to worry about him, going out to get news the way he'd done, but I had been fearful all the same.

"Any news, Father?" I asked as I slid into my seat, eying the scrumptious looking meal Collette had prepared for us.

"They're retreating," he said. He sounded almost dazed.

"What?" Alec and I said, staring open-mouthed at Father.

This was unbelievable.

"What caused their retreat?" I asked.

They had come to destroy our city. Take it over completely. Not kill a few Elf warriors then retreat, running back the way they'd come. Or so I had thought.

"We don't know. We didn't win the battle, that much is clear," Father answered, helping himself to the meat and vegetables lying in their dishes before us. He passed the steamed rice to Alec, shaking his head.

"Do you think this was just the first skirmish?" Alec asked. "Gorion testing our strength before laying the full might of his army upon us?"

Father shrugged.

"King Ethele and I have been guessing all afternoon as soon as we saw the army begin their retreat from the top of the palace's watchtower. King Ethele was commanding captains to report to the palace all day. There's been a steady influx of captains coming and going all afternoon, but they all say the same thing; they have no idea why Gorion would retreat suddenly like this."

He paused to take a bite of food.

"It's very mysterious," he continued. "We all thought he had come to lay waste to the city. That he would kill King Ethele, Prince Simone, and all eleven of us Lords of the Council. Take over being ruler of Karaphyllon. The council mentioned his rule of terror in the meetings. We all thought it would begin once the city fell."

He shook his head, as if he couldn't believe the strange, but relieving, turn of events.

"Now that Gorion is retreating, we don't know what he's planning next. I just wish there was some way we could find out," Father said.

My eyes widened in fear. Not knowing Gorion's next move was scary. We thought the city was doomed, that the fight with the army gathering at our door these past few weeks would be our last stand. I had hoped that we might prevail in the battle, but I hadn't expected this.

My hands that held my eating utensils trembled at the thought that perhaps, even now, Gorion was planning something even worse than overtaking the capital city of Karaphyllon and setting himself up as a tyrant, enslaving us all.

Alec sat, his plate of food untouched, his brow furrowed, deep in thought, staring at the flickering candle on the table. He chewed on his lip, then shook his head slowly, still staring at the candle. Then he looked up at Father and me.

"Do you think perhaps he discovered where Karaphyllon's Treasure is?" he asked, looking first at Father, then at me.

My eyes widened in horror at the thought. Karaphyllon's Treasure kept our world hidden and safe from other worlds and the evil that lay beyond our world. Without it, Karaphyllon would collapse as we knew it. If Gorion found the Treasure that King Ethele had hidden thousands of years ago when he ascended to the throne, we were all doomed. We might as well slit our own throats now then have Gorion take possession of our Treasure.

"No," Father breathed, his eyes wide in fear, his fork and knife hovering over his plate, forgotten.

"But that's got to be it," Alec said, speaking earnestly now. "There's nothing else in the world that would have him retreating like this. His scouts have found that Treasure and he's off to possess it for himself."

"What kind of power do you think the Treasure will give Gorion, if he steals it from us?" I asked, the truth of Alec's guess still sinking in. I suddenly felt sick to my stomach, as if I would vomit up the little bit of supper I'd already eaten. I hoped with everything in me that Alec was guessing wrong, that we were just speaking hypothetically.

"It's hard to say," Alec said. "No one has disturbed the Treasure for thousands of years. Not since King Ethele hid it when he first took the throne, over three thousand years ago now. It gave King Ethele wisdom to rule rightly and justly. It gave his father before him the strength to destroy the steel giants that came and waged war on Karaphyllon five thousand years ago. It gave the king before that the magic needed for blacksmithing and other forms of art." He said this with a nod at me. "The kings of Karaphyllon have passed down that Treasure for generations, ever since the Mighty One gave it to the first king ever to rule in Karaphyllon, back when He roamed this blessed land, before he went to await us in Sterathelassa." He bit his lip, thinking.

"Our Treasure is what's kept our land hidden and safe for thousands of years," Father added. "It's never been possessed by a being of pure evil like Gorion. Who knows what power the Treasure will give him if he has discovered its hiding place."

The Mighty One help us. I hoped Alec's guess at why Gorion was retreating was wrong.

CHAPTER 22

THE CERTIFICATE

Gwynneth

With Gorion's army on the retreat, there was nothing left to do but get me well enough to travel to Alec's manor in Annwythel. By this time, I had agreed to go. It would be good to meet his mother and sister, especially now that we were officially betrothed. It was the right thing to do.

I stopped trying to show I was stronger than I felt, and rested in my room whenever Alec urged me to, which was some mornings and every afternoon.

Two days after Gorion's army left the city, I was in my room when I heard a soft knock on my door. I got up to answer it and found Alec standing in the doorway. His smile lit up his tanned, handsome face, and I once again felt lucky to be betrothed to such a good-looking ellas. Even if I wasn't planning on marrying him.

"What is it?" I asked, too curious to return his smile.

"I know you're resting, but you need to come downstairs. You have a visitor."

"Who?" I wondered. We never had visitors to our house during these days of uncertainty.

"Come and find out," he said, his smile turning into a conspiratorial grin.

"You're really not going to tell me?" I asked, my curiosity growing as I felt a smile on my own lips. I peered down the stairwell, wondering who would want to see me, especially if they'd been told I was injured and resting.

All I got from Alec was a shake of his head, his mischievous grin still plastered on his face.

I sighed, and slowly made my way down the stairs.

"Who could want to see me?" I asked him in the stairwell.

Then I rounded the corner, stepped into the parlor, and there stood Master Carlel, still in his work clothes, looking out of place inside our nice house. He stood confidently smiling at me, his chest puffed out, pure pride on his face.

"Master Carlel, it's you," I greeted him. "I was wondering who'd come to pay me a visit. I'm glad you've come. Please, sit," I said, instantly taking up the role of hostess as I was used to doing when Father introduced me to his important guests from the palace.

All three of us took our seats, and there was a small, comfortable silence. The sun streaming through the windows had warmed the room and I could hear birds chattering in the garden outside.

"I'm glad you've stopped by." I fiddled with a throw pillow, too nervous to ask Carlel why he was here. I didn't want to get my hopes up just for him not to be finished writing up my certificate. "I don't think I've seen you step foot in this house since the day you agreed to take Timithen and I on as your apprentices." Perhaps if I mentioned my apprenticeship, it would loosen his tongue. He looked incredibly awkward sitting on our elaborate couch in his plain clothes.

"Well, seeing as you haven't been by the forge with your injury and all, I wanted to come by to deliver this." He pulled out an official-looking piece of paper from his pocket and handed it to me.

"Is this what I think it is?" I asked, staring at the folded paper, then looking questioningly up at him. I was too afraid to look at it.

"Open it and find out," he urged, smiling.

I opened it, and beamed. It was my certificate of apprenticeship. It stated that I'd completed my three-year apprenticeship and could now practice as a full-fledged blacksmith anywhere in Karaphyllon. The tears sprang to my eyes, and I gulped down the lump that was in my throat.

"Oh, Master Carlel, thank you," I breathed, looking up at him.

I'd never seen the old ellas look so proud. "Congratulations," he said warmly.

"Yes, congratulations, Gwynneth," Alec, sitting beside me, chimed in. "I know this means a lot to you."

"Oh, it means the world to me," I said, pressing my lips together, not able to tear my eyes from the words printed on the piece of paper. Those beautiful words that said I was worthy of an ellas's trade.

"Well, now that my task is done, I should get back to the forge," Carlel said, standing up to go.

"You won't stay and visit?" I asked, wishing he would say yes. With my apprenticeship being finished, there was no reason for me to go back to the forge. I didn't know when I would see him again.

"Can't spare the time, I'm afraid," he said. "Some other day, perhaps." And with that, he saw himself out.

I sat there in stunned silence, beaming at the certificate I held in my hands. I had done this; become a blacksmith. This was something I had worked hard for. Now, my hard work had paid off and I could set up my own forge anywhere I wanted. Perhaps in Annwythel, if Alec and I did marry in the end. He had already said that he would let me do something of the like, and I intended to take him up on his offer. Being a smithy was as natural to me as breathing after three long years of thinking of little else.

"How many more days before you think you can ride in a carriage the length of the trip to Annwythel?" Alec asked.

I looked over at him, blinking my eyes as I cleared my head of thoughts about the future.

"Hmm?" I asked almost dreamily, then considered his question.

I was still in considerable pain, but I knew how much he wanted us to leave the city. I knew how much I wanted to leave the city now, too. It was only a matter of time before the Throes came back to finish taking the city. If only we knew Gorion's plans for sure. I shuddered at the thought of those monsters entering my home, burning it to the ground.

"We can leave today if you want." I lifted my chin. The carriage ride would hurt, but it would be worth it to get away to safety. I couldn't fight anymore. If those Throes returned soon and found me, I would die, and I was too stubborn to give up my life that easily.

Alec nodded, looking worried. "The sooner we can get on the road, the better. I'm afraid of Gorion and his army returning."

"As am I," I answered, thinking back to that horrible day of battling the Throes and the awful moment when they'd injured me. My injuries burned like fire as I relived the pain of receiving them. "But I'm glad we stayed long enough for me to receive this." I indicated my certificate. I couldn't take my eyes off it. This accomplishment made me very proud.

"I'm sorry, Gwynneth," he said, after a moment's pause. "I should have offered you a chance to finish after the battle was over. Forgive me."

I pursed my lips and didn't reply. It was a hard thing to forgive. I was glad that he was thinking about what he had asked me to give up when he'd demanded I leave the city before the battle, and that he was sorry for it now.

"It's alright," I said, doing the gallant thing and forgiving him. "Why do you think his army is going to return?" I changed the subject, wondering if he'd heard more information from the council.

"They didn't finish the job they came here to do. They didn't take the city," he stated, shifting in his place on the couch.

"Perhaps they have a different objective now and we won't be seeing them again," I said optimistically.

"I only wish we knew for sure," he said. "I hope I'm wrong that he's after the Treasure. If only we could figure out how to be rid of the threat of Gorion." He said this last sentence quieter, his voice sounding worried, as if Gorion was often heavy on his mind and he was at an utter loss as to what to do. He shook his head, frowning. "If only."

I sighed, wishing he would get his mind off Gorion and the awful threat of his army. But Alec was a Lord of the Council, and this threat to our country's safety was his job to take care of.

"Well," I said, rising from my seat and heading toward the door. "If we're leaving today, I'd better pack."

"Are you sure you feel well enough to travel today?" he asked, his voice dripping with concern.

I turned back around to face him, touched at how worried his face looked. "Of course I feel well enough for it." I answered him with a reassuring smile. "I may be stiff, but I am getting better. You shouldn't worry about me so much."

He stood up and walked over to stand next to me, putting his arm on the doorframe to stop me, looking down at me earnestly.

"I wouldn't worry about you so much if I knew you were the type of ellassen to rest like you're told. But I know you well enough, Gwynneth, to know that you push yourself too hard. So please, for my sake, don't overdo it?" he asked softly, his eyes warm.

"I promise," I answered as butterflies churned in my stomach.

Oh, the way he was looking at me was enough to take my breath away. I swallowed, and ducked under his arm to scurry off to my bedroom. I needed to keep my hands busy, to get my mind off Alec and my blacksmith's certificate. If I was left alone with my thoughts, they would whirl back and forth in confusion between Alec and the certificate I had left in the parlor. What my future held, I didn't know, and that's what scared me the most, the uncertainty of it all. So, I worked, despite the pain.

Alec was handsome, yes, that was a fact that I couldn't deny. But he was just like Father, wanting his will for me over my own. I didn't know if I could willingly put myself under such a man. Perhaps he was different in normal circumstances. Perhaps he wasn't always like this. But this was wartime, and he was being overly protective of me, like he should be, I knew, but it was still hard to face.

I knew deep down all he wanted was for me to be safe, to be far away from the battles that raged in our land, away from danger and harm. Was that a sign that he truly cared for me and that he would take care of me? I didn't know. I felt as if I knew nothing of ellases, nothing but the example my father was for me.

Father has been a good example of the typical ellas. But I also felt that I hadn't paid enough attention to others who had crossed my path my whole life. I didn't know how to judge an ellas, and I didn't know the right decision to make in this, my betrothal to Alec. I felt at such a loss.

Shaking myself out of my reverie, I began singing softly to myself, anything to keep my mind off Alec and everything having to do with my betrothal.

CHAPTER 23

The Journey to Annwythel

Gwynneth

During the midday meal, I stated that I had healed enough from my injuries to make the trip to Annwythel. I was still sore and knew the journey would be uncomfortable, but I was ready to get a move on. It did no good sitting still, cooped up in our house, waiting for Gorion to return with his army and finish wiping Trescone off the map.

Alec looked at me and smiled. "Good." His blue eyes shone, though I saw a hint of worry behind his smile. "I'm excited for you to meet my mother and sister. You'll like them, I'm sure."

"I hope so," I answered patronizingly.

He hadn't told me much about them other than that I would like them, and I had my doubts. I only hoped they turned out to be as nice as Alec. If that was true, then I would like them, but I was nervous to meet them.

The journey to Annwythel would take us three days by carriage, and I was eager to get it over with. I'd had a few days for my injuries to heal, but I knew the jolting carriage would cause my wounds to ache. I wished to get the journey done with as soon as possible.

"We'll plan on you two leaving tomorrow morning, then," Father decided.

"Is there no way we could leave today?" I wanted to know, eager to leave. If I was going to put my beloved city behind me and see what it would be like to become Alec's bride in a year, it was now or never.

"I'm sure you have a lot of packing to do, daughter," Father was quick to answer. "You're going to a lord's house for a length of some months. You'll need to pack sufficiently, so you don't arrive there unprepared."

"I've already begun packing, Father," I said with a proud smile.

"Have Collette help you finish, please. I don't want you to forget anything important."

"Yes, Father," I hastily agreed, looking down at my plate. I felt the tips of my ears burn as I realized he was right. It would take me all day to finish packing for this journey if he expected me to dress like a lord's daughter while at Annwythel.

"Tomorrow it is then," Father reemphasized with a smile.

It was still dark when I heard the knock on my door early the next morning, the signal that I was to rise and prepare to leave in the carriage. I quickly dressed in a lavender wool traveling dress and pulled a gray cardigan over it, as it was still chilly this fall morning. I fastened the hooks on my high-top traveling shoes as quickly as I could, but with so many, it still took longer than I liked. Finished, I grabbed my little satchel to carry with me in the carriage seat and stepped out of my bedroom door.

Father and Alec stood at the bottom of the stairs, waiting for me.

I went straight to Father and gave him a hug, not trusting my voice to be steady enough to tell him my goodbyes using words. This was the first time I would be separated from Father since Mother and Timithen died. My throat was tight, and I felt the tears springing to my eyes.

Blink them away. I told myself. *This is stupid. You won't miss him this much, will you?*

But in my heart, I knew I would. Though Father was responsible for a lot of my misery these past weeks, he was the only family I had, and I knew I would be homesick for him in the weeks to come. Hopefully, we would exchange letters, but even the mail was slow.

I turned from Father to Alec. The smile he gave me friendly, and a little unsure about where we stood in our relationship, made me feel sorry for him. Had I been treating him that harshly?

I wasn't expecting this turn of events in the past few weeks involving him, and I hadn't taken it well. Perhaps I had been too hard on him. Perhaps I should have given him more of a chance. We were betrothed now, after all. Perhaps I should open my heart to the possibility of finding love. I didn't know. I knew nothing about ellases. No one had ever liked me like Alec did; all of this was new and strange. I was afraid. There, I said it. I was afraid to open my heart to him, afraid that I would get hurt.

"Ready?" he asked me, still smiling.

"Yes," I replied, deciding to give him half a chance, and smiled back at him.

We went outside into the cool morning air. The sun was just peeping over the city, the white walls bathed in orange. With the sun, came the warmth for the day. Our carriage awaited us on the lonely street. The lampposts were still lit, dotting the walkway of each noble's home. The coachman hopped down from his seat and came around to open the door, offering his hand to help me in.

I was caught off guard when I realized Alec had stepped in and it was his hand I was taking to be helped into the carriage, not the coachman's. Blushing at the sudden touch that sent butterflies into my stomach as soon as I realized it was him, I hastily got into the coach. The faster I quit holding his hand, the better. He released my hand as

I settled into my seat, and I idly wiped it on my skirt. He quickly got in beside me.

I thought he would be like my father when we rode in a carriage together, and sit across from me, but no. He took his seat beside me on the bench, as if it was the most natural thing in the world that we should sit beside each other as we traveled.

Swallowing hard, I willed myself not to stare at him in shock but looked out the window. Father was standing underneath the colonnade anyway and I should wave to him.

Alec knocked on the roof of the carriage to let the coachman sitting above us know we were ready to go, and the carriage jolted into motion. I waved to Father, the realization that I was leaving home for a long time hitting me like a slap. The thought made me so cold that I shivered and pulled my cardigan tighter around me. I was going away from my home with no set date to return. As long as the capital was under threat from Gorion, Father wouldn't let me return until he knew it was safe.

I watched Father waving regally back at me as the carriage pulled away and he got smaller and smaller. I wondered how long it would be until I would see him again, the only family I had left in the world.

Our carriage took us to the coach station where we waited the few minutes it took for our baggage to be loaded and for the proper time for the coach to set off from Trescone.

The coach station was lonely. It looked like everyone who had wanted to leave Trescone had already done so. We were the only two travelers when our coach took off, headed down the quiet streets and out of the main gates.

"Excited?" Alec asked after a few moments of riding in silence through the countryside.

I pulled away from staring out the window, and looked at his expectant face.

"No," I said, deciding it was better to be honest with him than to pretend that I was what he wanted me to be.

His face fell, and he looked down at his hands. "Why not?" he ventured after a moment or two, looking over at me. His voice told me he was afraid to ask the question.

"I-I'm mostly just nervous," I answered carefully, looking up at him, still a little wary to open up to him.

"Nervous about meeting my family?" he pressed gently, his blue eyes caring and heartfelt.

I nodded. "You haven't told me much about them in these two weeks," I pointed out. "Perhaps if you told me a bit about them, I would feel more comfortable." I tried to sound helpful because I did wish to know more about his family before I met them.

"What would you like to know about them?" he asked innocently, as if the thought of telling me about them hadn't even entered his mind.

"Well, perhaps something more than 'I'm excited for you to meet my family. I'm sure you'll like them,'" I said, smiling as I repeated the words he'd spoken to me on more than one occasion.

He smiled at that, giving a short breathy laugh, recognizing his own words being thrown back at him in such a teasing manner.

"I see," he said, then told me a bit more about his mother and sister who lived with him at Annwythel Manor.

We traveled along for several hours, talking pleasantly as the sun rose higher in the sky and the day became warmer. I shed my cardigan after a while, and still we continued talking, not once mentioning our betrothal, or the battle we'd fought, my injuries, or my father's and his expectations for me. It was nice to be talking about different subjects, and I felt myself relaxing in his presence actually enjoying myself. It was a good feeling.

⸺❖⸺

We were traveling along the morning of our second day on the road, when the coachman called down below, "Throes ahead!"

Instantly, I was on the alert. My body tensed, preparing for action, and I looked about the carriage for a weapon of sorts. Alec was just as tense as he stood and took the cushion off the seat across from us, pulling out a sword from a small space built into the seat and handing it to me.

"Here, you'll need this," he said, then took one out for himself as well. He gave me a wry, reassuring smile, as if he knew I could handle whatever was going to come next. "What's the plan?" he called up to the coachman, who hadn't slowed down his pace.

"Speed up. Try to outrun them," the coachman called down. "I don't think they're as fast as we are."

"Let's do it," Alec said with a determined nod.

The coachman whipped up the horses, and soon we were going faster than I'd ever ridden in a coach before. The wind from the open windows whipped through my loose hair, tossing it this way and that. I gripped my sword as I saw the wicked-looking Throes grow larger and larger as we approached them. They were standing in the middle of the road, barring our way. There was no way we could take the coach off the road and around them. Going right through was our only chance.

"I'd like some more cover up here!" the coachman called down to Alec. Right now, there was only the coachman and his baggage ellas up top to defend against the monsters. They were probably both armed, but still, if the Throes attacked anywhere, it would be up top. It was way easier to climb up there than to get in through the doors down here.

"Right," Alec said. "Gwynneth, you're in charge down here. Take out any Throes that climb in through the doors. Got it?"

I nodded, my mouth too dry to form words. That Alec trusted my skill with a sword enough that he would leave me by myself in this part of the carriage spoke volumes. He must have watched me fight in the battle at Trescone far longer than I thought he had.

With that, Alec sheathed his sword and made his way through the little skylight hole to the top of the coach.

I sat down on the bench and watched as we approached the monsters. The pace the coach was going was too fast to balance very well while standing.

The Throes got closer and closer. I could see them brandishing their swords and shouting in their obscene tongue, the words guttural, harsh, and cruel. If only we could make out of this alive and with our coach intact.

CHAPTER 24

The End of the Journey

Gwynneth

Then we were charging through the ranks of Throes. The horses trampled a few, but most jumped out of the way, then leaped toward our carriage, snarling viciously, black swords in hand.

I heard the thuds of several of them land on the roof, then screamed as an ugly head appeared in the window, the Throe's hands clutching to the inside of the carriage, fumbling for the door handle.

Standing and balancing in the moving carriage as best I could, I brought my sword down on its wrists as hard as I could, metal meeting flesh.

The creature roared in pain, snapping at me with his fangs. I heard the din of the battle going on up top, but had no time to think about how Alec and the coachmen were faring. I brought my sword down on the creature's wrists again and again, anything to loosen its grip on our carriage so it would fall off.

Instead, it seemed to have found its footing on the coach step below, its head raising a few inches higher as it pressed its face deeper into the carriage. It seemed unphased by its partially hacked off hands, the red bloodlust of battle rage in its animal-like eyes.

My heart pounded in my chest, and I willed myself to hold my sword steady. I would not let this creature kill me. Not if I could help it.

It kept snapping its fangs at me, biding its time until I got too close to it and it could rip my throat out with its wolf-like capabilities. I kept my distance, glad that my reach with my sword was longer than its reach with its snarling, snapping fangs.

Then I saw my chance and drove my sword into its wide open mouth, pushing it as far back as I could. The monster tried closing its jaws around my sword, thrashing this way and that, anything to wrest the weapon from my grasp. I grabbed my sword with both hands and pulled it out. With a sweeping arc of my sword, I hacked off its head. It let go of the carriage and dropped to the ground, bouncing and rolling several times as we sped away before it came to a stop.

I fell back onto the coach seat, breathing hard, my heart filled with relief.

I had done my part. I had held my own and felt very proud of myself. Once again, I had proved my metal.

I didn't hear signs of a struggle up top anymore, so I stepped onto the coach seat and popped my head through the opening Alec had disappeared through.

"Everything all right up here?" I looked around and saw Alec helping the baggage ellas from the strongbox that held our luggage back into the driver's box. The baggage ellas was holding a white scarf to his arm, which was quickly turning red with his blood.

"We're fine," Alec said, dropping into the driver's box and helping to ease the ellas into the seat beside him. He turned around to look at me, his eyes filled with concern. "And you? Are you all right?" His voice was tight, his lips one long, thin line.

I gave him a reassuring smile. "I'm fine."

"You don't look fine," he said, his eyes wild. "You've got black blood splattered all over your face and neck." He tossed me a handkerchief. "Just tell me you gave that Throe what he deserved and then some."

"All right. I will," I said, grinning.

He turned back to the baggage ellas. "I'll be down as soon as I can get Finley patched up here."

I nodded and plopped back down on the seat cushions. The adrenaline slowly seeped out of my system, making my legs and arms feel weak as a babe's. I rested my head back on the cushions, glad that was over.

Alec came down a few minutes later and put a comforting arm around my shoulders.

I jumped at the sudden, unexpected touch but decided to allow it. It felt reassuring to have his arm about my shoulders, silently telling me we were out of danger and they hadn't harmed us.

"I'm happy that's over," I said, leaning into him, needing his strength.

"Me, too," he murmured. "I was very afraid for us back there. I don't know what we would have done if they'd killed one of us."

"I'm just glad we were strong enough to fight back. I mean, four of us against thirty of them?" I shook my head in disbelief. "What are the odds that we would come out nearly unscathed?"

He nodded. "We should thank the Mighty One for sparing our lives."

"How is Finley faring?"

He shrugged. "He'll mend. I don't think their swords have poisoned tips. I just don't know what these Throes were doing this far south. We heard the rest of their army was traveling north, toward the great mountain ranges." As he said this, I saw a sliver of worry come into his eyes, but he blinked the expression away.

"Do we know what they plan to do, going to the Northern Mountains like that? There's nothing out that way, it's just a wilderness."

"I only know of one thing out in the Northern Mountains, and I pray the Mighty One that they don't get it," he said, then bit his lip and looked away, as if he had said too much.

"What's out in the Northern Mountains?" I pressed him, my curiosity peeked.

"I...I want to wait until we get to Annwythel. So, I can tell both you and my family at the same time," he said, meeting my eyes. The stark blue of his own eyes was serious.

"Alright, sounds fair enough," I said, wondering what he had to say about it all.

Guess it would have to wait until we arrived safely at Annwythel. I hoped to the Mighty One that we would arrive safely at Alec's home. If there was one party of Throes lurking about not where they were supposed to be, no doubt there were more. How this band had slipped through our Elvish spy defenses unspotted, worried me.

We traveled on, ever more wary of the road before us.

⸺⊰✦⊱⸺

Alec

I needed to tell her. Tell her the truth about my family, once and for all.

When I'd handed her that sword, my hand had trembled. I hadn't wanted to hand her that sword, hadn't wanted to see what death she could wield with it. But I'd seen her in the battle of Trescone, knew she was good with a blade. Knew I could trust her, the way I couldn't trust Mirith.

I looked over at her sitting beside me, staring out the window. She needed to know. I hadn't even told her father yet. Someone from her family needed to know before this betrothal went on any further.

"I need to tell you something," I said, my voice nearly a whisper as I choked on the words.

She looked over at me. "Alright."

Her smile lit up her face. Once again, I marveled at the way she always brought sunshine and life when she smiled at me. I pressed my lips together and was quiet for a minute or two. I was afraid to tell her the truth, so afraid.

She placed a hand on my arm. "Alec, I'm your be-trothed," she pressed me, when I couldn't form the words that were on the tip of my tongue. The silence was stifling. "You can tell me anything. I hope you know that." Her voice was gentle, trustworthy.

"I know," I said, my voice tight. Turning to her, I knew she saw the agony on my face, and yet she waited patiently for me to tell her about it. "When my father died," I began. I hesitated, then started over. "I suppose I need to tell you how my father died." I bit my lip and took her left hand in mine, interlacing our fingers. Her touch was what I needed right now, anything to reassure myself. "My sister killed him," I said, and she reeled back, horrified at the revelation.

"What! What do you mean?" she exclaimed. She swallowed, and waited for me to explain.

"It was an accident," I said, trying to reassure her. I couldn't have her lose faith with my family. Not now. "An accident with a sword," I sighed, and went on, squeezing her hand harder now as I told the story.

"We were all there, Mother, Father, me, and my sister, Mirith. We were in our weapons room. Father was showing us the new sword that King Ethele had recently decorated him with. Mirith was only eleven, not old enough to be responsible in the weapons room. When you see the weapons room, you'll understand how she got hold of a weapon and accidentally hurt someone with it.

"Father kept all his most valuable, and often his sharpest, weapons, on display in his weapons room. Father was showing Mother and me the fine details of the sword he'd just received and telling us the story of how King Ethele presented it to him with all the pomp and circumstance the king enjoys doing. Mirith wandered off from the rest of us.

"Another weapon caught her eye. A retractable sword. She picked it up from its display. Father saw her and moved toward her to take the sword.

"'No, Mirith!' he shouted at her. She turned toward him and pushed the button for the sword to extend. It extended, right into Father's gut. Mirith dropped it, horrified at what she'd done, but it was too late. Father crumpled to the floor, bleeding out. Mother ran to go get help, but by the time she came back, it was too late. She found Mirith and me kneeling at Father's side. He was already gone. Just like that. In a matter of minutes."

I shook my head at the memory, knowing my face was white as I relived the story. It had been brutal. And quick.

"There was nothing any of us could have done differently, not after that sword pierced my father." I clutched both her hands in mine now, reaching for a lifeline.

"I needed to tell you because—well, I haven't told anyone, not even your father. No one on the council knows, either. Mother somehow kept it a secret from everybody. I don't know how she did it. Maybe she was afraid that if other Elves knew the truth, they'd do something to Mirith. Put her in prison, or kill her for murdering her own father in cold blood."

"But it was an accident," she pointed out.

"Yes," I said, my face becoming tight as I pressed my lips together again. "But if we're going to marry, I needed to tell you. Get it off my chest."

"Thank you for telling me," she said, giving my hand a squeeze and smiling at me reassuringly. "I'm sorry. Sorry that you had to live through that. It must have been awful."

"It was more than awful," I was quick to say. "I became a lord at his death and have been trying to live up to his reputation ever since. All while hiding how he died." I shot her a glimmer of a smile, then looked out the carriage window.

There. I'd told her. I'd done it. There was no more to say.

She must have sensed I didn't wish to speak of it any further as she remained quiet beside me, looking out the carriage window as well.

⸺⟐⸺

Gwynneth

We rode in silence for some time, the day growing ever warmer and not a cloud to be seen in the great expanse of the blue sky. All around us were fields as far as the eye could see. There were no trees, except for the few around each farmhouse to shelter it from the wind.

I felt honored that Alec would trust me with such a deep, dark secret as the one he'd just shared. How many weeks had he been looking at me, wondering what I'd think if he told me? Too many, by the looks of how he sat with his eyes glued to the window outside, his hands balled into fists at his sides. It had taken every ounce of courage he had to tell me something like that. And I liked him for being vulnerable with me.

Occasionally we saw workers out in the fields, Elves of a lower rank than us who had to work for their living. Having completed an apprenticeship myself, I felt as if I could relate to them. I knew what it was to work with my hands, to reap the rewards of my labor, to find pride in my work. It's a satisfactory feeling to work and accomplish things in this long life we have here in Karaphyllon.

Elves are eternal beings. We only die if someone or something kills us. But no matter if we live an eternity or die a cruel death, we all end up in the same place: Sterathelassa, the Land Beyond the Sea. It is our one great dream, to go to our final home there and live with the Mighty One forever in perfect peace and rest. Sterathelassa is often in my waking dreams during my night's rest. Those are the nights when I feel most peaceful and when I wake up in the morning most refreshed.

I smiled at the memories of those beautiful dreams of Sterathelassa, quite content, as we continued our journey to Annwythel.

⸺◈⸺

We saw no more Throes all the rest of our journey that day. It was peaceful driving through the countryside, quiet. The fields in this part of Karaphyllon stretched on into the horizon. Trees dotted the few lone farmhouses and surrounded the scant villages we passed through. Other than that, it was wide open sky, bright blue days, and golden fields ripe with the harvest.

I grew ever more nervous as we came closer and closer to Annwythel Manor. Alec spent several hours telling me a little about his family, but I still felt apprehensive at the thought of meeting them this soon.

Then the morning of the day we were to arrive dawned.

My heart thumped in my chest and my palms felt sweaty as the carriage drove toward Annwythel Manor. I'd never thought I would be nervous about meeting Alec's family. It was because I wasn't sure if I wanted to marry him. I'd only known him a few weeks. But our fate was practically sealed. There was almost no turning back now, not unless we wanted to be the talk of the nobility. How much would it devastate our families if I broke it off in the end?

If I ended up not marrying him I would still be happy. I had finished my apprenticeship now, and gotten my certificate. I could open my own blacksmith shop anywhere in Karaphyllon.

Yet still, my heart was pounding in my chest. Alec said it was only about a mile until we were there. What would his mother and sister think of me? I hoped they would like me. Alec thought they would. Yet, despite everything he'd told me about them, I still had my doubts. I wondered how much he had told them about me. Hopefully enough to make them like me.

The horses covered the last mile quickly, and we came into view of the house. Mansion was the correct word for it. I gasped. It was even larger than my home in Trescone.

A long, cobblestone drive, blocked off by a black iron gate, led up to a three-story mansion built out of white stone. An ivy-covered turret rose on the left side of the house several stories above the rest of the building. Black shutters covered the many windows on the front of the mansion, opened to let in the afternoon sunlight. Huge black double doors made up the entrance. The manor house was gorgeous. What extravagance!

If I married Alec, I would live here one day. How fortunate was I? How could I even contemplate not marrying him now?

He was a Lord of Karaphyllon and ruled the entire province of Annwythel. An eligible man of power, not to mention his good looks.

I stole a quick glance at Alec. He gave me a proud, yet humble smile and grabbed my hand. I must have looked nervous.

"They'll love you, Gwynneth," he said. "I promise."

END OF BOOK ONE

Join Claudia Klein's Newsletter

Want to get the prequel novella ebook to *Song of Siege and Shadows* for free? Join my author newsletter to receive *Court of Shadows and Games*, the prequell novella that begins this series. Along with your ebook you'll also receive access to: book deals, free book alerts, giveaways, announcements about my next book before everyone else hears them, occasional exclusive short stories from me, and more as part of being subscribed to my newsletter.

You can join my newsletter and download your free ebook by scanning this QR code:

ACKNOWLEDGEMENTS

It's always fun creating a new book. The process of writing, editing, formatting, and publishing is one of my favorite things to do. I absolutely love that I've made my little hobby of writing stories a career. How cool is that? I get to do what I love every day, all thanks to you, my dear readers.

Thank you so much for coming along on Gwynneth's journey. I hope you've enjoyed the story. There's more to come. Are you ready for it?

Creating a book wouldn't be possible without the help of a lot of people. Here are few that come to mind.

Thanks so much to my lovely editor, Alena Orrison. Your work was once again, outstanding. I'm so glad to have you as my editor.

Thank you to my cover designer, Mia from CoverLove Graphic Designs. You did such a fabulous job with the cover. I'm excited to see what you can create for the rest of the series.

Thank you to my beta readers, Kristin, Bethany, and Chelsea. Your enthusiasm for this book was what kept me going during the editing process. Thank you so much for your excitement about the plotline, the long conversations about the book, and all your suggestions on how to make the story better.

Thank you to my husband, who lets me do this work as my fulltime job. Your support of this little career of mine is beautiful and I am very grateful. I know there are a lot of writers who don't have the support of their loved ones.

Thank you to my kids, who keep me on my toes. You guys remind me what life is like without worries. I love going on adventures with you.

Thank you to my Heavenly Father who continues to bless this little venture of mine.

Let's go get lost in another good book, shall we?

About the Author

Claudia Klein began writing as soon as she could spell. She began her first full length fantasy novel in high school soon after reading The Lord of the Rings for the first time for British Literature class. She's been writing fantasy ever since. Though she didn't study writing in college, she founded a women's writing club for the women of her university. Soon after college she was introduced to the Indie author world and knew it was for her. She's been publishing her books ever since.

OTHER WORKS

Did you like this story? Check out Claudia Klein's other novels at claudiakleinauthor.com

www.ingramcontent.com/pod-product-compliance
Lightning Source LLC
Chambersburg PA
CBHW032023310726
48972CB00002B/525